"What are you doing here?" Ivy asked

"Answer me," Linc snapped. "Is the baby all right?"

Confusion darted over her face. "Why do you care?"

His eyes widened. "Why do I care? It's my child."

"You don't know that!"

For a shocked second he actually considered that the child might not be his. It didn't last. "No," he said, shaking his head. "You're not like that. You wouldn't go to another man's bed after we—"

Hectic color rose in her cheeks. "Why not? You did." She whirled toward the kitchen.

Linc recoiled and almost let her get away. He grabbed her arm. "You don't understand," he began.

She didn't wait to hear. "I understand plenty," she said, trying to free her arm. "You came here, you lied to all of us, you wormed your way into our confidence and then you—" Her voice wavered as memories of that night rose before her eyes.

She tugged again, but he wouldn't let her go, afraid that if she got away from him he'd never have another chance....

Dear Reader,

This is my seventh book, but my first Superromance novel, and I'm thrilled to join such a wonderful group of authors and have a chance to tell you a story that's dear to my heart.

I'm a fifth-generation Texan who grew up in a small town; I've known and loved ornery old men like Carl (*ornery* is a term of fondness where I'm from) and feisty pioneer women like Aunt Prudie. I come from a long line of women with a treasured quality called "grit," translated as a core of strength to endure hardship with grace and heart. The "picket house" in which Carl lives actually exists and once belonged to my pioneer forebears; the stories Carl tells about Palo Verde's past are from research into my mother's family.

Palo Verde is modeled after the real town of Palo Pinto, where I had a delicious meal at the Palo Pinto Café, the inspiration for Ivy's café. Palo Pinto faced its own tough times, but the lovely people there have made Ivy's ideas a reality. More and more tourists are discovering the town and the beauty around it.

Above all, however, this story is about family, whether of blood or of the heart. Both Linc and Ivy lost theirs, and each chose a different path. Linc thinks he doesn't need a family; Ivy creates one everywhere she goes. It's also a story of how one person can make a difference in the lives of so many more.

So thank you for being here. Settle back, get comfy and let me tell you a story....

Jean

P.S. I love hearing from readers. You can reach me at P.O. Box 40012, Georgetown, TX 78628 or via the Internet at my Web site, www.jeanbrashear.com or at www.eHarlequin.com.

What the Heart Wants
Jean Brashear

HARLEQUIN®

TORONTO • NEW YORK • LONDON
AMSTERDAM • PARIS • SYDNEY • HAMBURG
STOCKHOLM • ATHENS • TOKYO • MILAN • MADRID
PRAGUE • WARSAW • BUDAPEST • AUCKLAND

ISBN 0-373-71071-2

WHAT THE HEART WANTS

For Katie
Beloved daughter of my own beloved daughter
New and precious link in a long chain of women with grit

CHAPTER ONE

"ONE OF THESE DAYS, this whole place is gonna come tumbling down," the old man muttered as he entered the Palo Verde Café.

"Good afternoon, Carl." Ivy Parker glanced around at the pots and bowls brimming with rainwater from leaks in the roof. "I could write another letter to the landlord," she said, kissing the hand of the dark-haired toddler in her arms. "Want to help me, Stevie?" she asked the child.

"Might as well let her help," Carl grumbled. "Nothing else is working. What are you doing with her again, anyway? You don't have enough to do, running the diner and playing nursemaid to your aunt? I don't believe you've sat down for more than five minutes since you moved here." He stopped suddenly and sniffed. "That apple pie I smell?"

Ivy grinned, shooting a glance at the train clock hanging on the ancient flowered wallpaper. Replacing the paper was on her list of to-dos. "Yes, and there's pecan waiting to bake. After I fix you a lunch plate, you're welcome to a piece." She handed Stevie to him. "Hold her for a minute while I switch the pies, will you, please?"

Carl glowered as she placed the little girl in his arms. "I do handyman tasks, missy—I ain't no baby-sitter. You're the one who takes on other people's kids and ever' lost soul you encounter. Ought to be raising babies of your own."

Ivy caught her breath. He didn't know that dream was gone now. She was here in Palo Verde to start over.

She reached for her pot holders and opened the oven door. "Stop fussing, Carl. Any man with seven grandkids can hold a baby for five minutes." She put the apple pies on racks to cool, then replaced them with the pecan. That done, she busied herself filling a plate for him from pots on the stove, then returned to the main dining area.

"Smells powerful good." Carl handed her the baby in exchange for the plate and settled into one of the booths she'd reupholstered in a sunny-blue vinyl. "After I finish the kitchen faucet, I'm climbing up on the roof."

"No, you're not."

"I may be older than dirt, but I ain't forgotten how to climb a ladder, young lady."

"You're not old, but it's not your responsibility."

"Not yours, either. It's that cheapskate's."

"But that cheapskate isn't answering my letters. I don't even know the cheapskate's name."

"It can't wait much longer, Ivy. And there's no one else around to do it."

"I don't want to argue with you anymore, Carl."

"Then, don't," he muttered.

She sighed. "For now, you eat." Ivy drew great pleasure from watching people eat her cooking, and their little trade suited them both. Carl hadn't done well after his wife Mildred died. Now Ivy knew that he was getting at least one good meal a day. Sometimes she had to make up things for him to do in return for food, but he was a proud man who wouldn't take charity. His Social Security didn't stretch far, so she liked being able to lend a hand.

"When's Sally coming back to get this baby? Seems like you got the child more than she does." He harrumphed. "When are you gonna take care of Ivy, instead of ever' other living soul you meet?"

"I'm doing fine." Thinking about herself just opened wounds. Better to be doing something productive. Great-aunt Prudie's need for assistance couldn't have come at a better time.

"Fine? You're busy every second of the day,

and now I hear that you're organizing a merchants' association. Revive Palo Verde?" He shook his head. "This town's been dead for years."

"There's a rich history here. This was once the biggest town in the county."

"And now it's deader than a doornail." He gestured out the window to the buildings that formed three sides of a town square, with the highway to Fort Worth making the fourth. "Half these buildings are in as bad a shape as this diner, and they all got the same landlord—who don't give a rat's patootie what happens to Palo Verde, I might add."

Ivy looked into Stevie's brown eyes and nibbled on her tiny fingers. Stevie gurgled with delight. "If we don't try, Carl, then children like this will have to move away when they grow up, just the way your kids did. There won't be any jobs." She glanced out the window and noticed an ancient pickup pulling up out front.

He snorted. "Ain't no jobs now, 'cept at the courthouse. Heck, next they'll probably vote to move the county seat."

"I have an idea that might help. A proposal for the landlord."

"*If* you can ever get an answer."

Ivy resisted a sigh, pushing back an errant lock of her hair. "If only I knew more about how to find the name of the real person behind that post office box. Maybe I need to take a trip to Dallas and see if I can discover anything useful.''

Carl's voice was gentle. ''Don't get your hopes up, Ivy girl. Even if you find him, no big-city company's gonna see any potential in this one-horse town.''

The screen door squeaked as it opened, and they both turned.

A dark-haired man stood in the doorway, his broad shoulders filling the frame.

Ivy couldn't help staring. His face, harsh planes and strong angles, wasn't so much handsome as noble. Even clad in worn jeans, he carried himself with pride. There was a sense about him that he'd known better times.

But not recently. He looked tired…soul weary, somehow. Between his dark brows, two lines dug deep grooves. Life hadn't gone easy on him, she could see. ''Are you here to eat?'' she asked. ''I'm afraid we're not open for dinner, only breakfast and lunch.''

He was silent, his gaze flickering around the room before finally settling on her.

''Are you all right?'' she prodded.

He seemed ill at ease. ''I was wondering if you could use a spare hand.''

"Oh, my—" Ivy and Carl traded astonished glances. The answer to a prayer, she thought.

Carl wasn't so eager. "You got any experience?"

The man's brows snapped together. "I know my way around a construction site."

"That don't mean—"

Ivy interrupted. "What Carl's trying to say is that our particular concern at the moment is, as you can see—" she pointed to the receptacles around her, which brimmed with rainwater "—the roof." Realizing Carl was right, if not diplomatic, she pressed on. "Have you had any roofing experience?"

"Yes." Nothing more. Just yes, as if his word were enough.

"I'm afraid I can't afford to pay much."

"I don't need much," he answered.

Ivy disagreed. He needed feeding. Looked as though he needed a friend. "Would you like something to eat? I have some leftovers. Or a piece of pie?"

When he didn't respond, she rushed to dispel any worries. "It's not—I won't charge you."

The stranger bristled. "I don't want handouts."

"I'm sorry. I didn't mean to offend you. I just thought—"

"What she means," Carl interrupted, "is that

Ivy here never met a lost soul she didn't want to adopt. You a lost soul, boy?''

"Not the last time I looked." Lincoln Galloway III had to work to keep the astonishment out of his face. *This* was the letter writer, Ivy Parker?

He had come to find the blue-haired crackpot who'd written all the letters on old-fashioned stationery in a delicate, feminine hand. He'd expected someone old enough to be his grandmother—nothing like the woman who stood before him.

Golden-haired with startling blue eyes, Ivy Parker couldn't be much more than thirty, too wholesome to be real, her face bright with color as thick dark eyelashes swept down to shadow her cheeks.

"Offer to climb that roof, boy, and look it over. Be a free meal, for sure—best one you ever had." The old man grinned. "Ivy thinks I don't know she's scared for me to get on that ladder. Thinks I'm too old." He shrugged. "Probably am, but up to now, no one better showed." He snorted in derision. "Sure thing that worthless landlord ain't going to bother."

Linc flinched inwardly. The "worthless landlord" had been his brother, Garner. He glanced around at the pots and bowls on the floor, debris that was evidence of his brother's mistakes. *His* mistakes. Untangling the frayed ends of Garner's life would be his penance. He would start here, with this roof. The job would provide him with a closer, covert examination of the properties that were all that was left to Garner's widow. "I could take a look at it for you. A piece of pie sounds fine."

"I'd do it, but even if I knew anything about roofs, I'm just a little afraid of heights." She said it as though confessing to a sin.

"Heights don't bother me."

"Oh, if you wouldn't mind, that would be a godsend." Her smile was wide and lovely, dazzling and so different from that of the nipped, tucked and tanned women of his acquaintanceship. Her honey-blond hair escaped from her ponytail; flour dusted one cheek.

She smelled of cinnamon and flowers.

Linc shook his head to clear it. He hadn't known women like her still existed. The dark-haired toddler in her arms had a death grip on the pale-pink fabric of her dress. She'd make hot chocolate and cookies for that child in winter, tell stories every night. Squeeze fresh lemonade to take on picnics in summer.

Lucky kid.

"I'm Ivy Parker and this is Carl Thompson." She held out a slim hand.

He took it, surprised by the firm clasp, the small calluses. Her nails were short and unpainted.

His women tended more toward scarlet claws.

"Linc…Garner." With an unexpected twinge over his subterfuge, he let her go. "Pleased to meet you," he said, shaking the old man's hand.

"Where are you from, Linc?" she asked.

"Here and there."

The old man frowned, but Ivy leaped into the breach. "Well, just have a seat anywhere. I'll be back in a jiff. Would you like coffee with your pie? Iced tea?"

"Iced tea. Don't you want me to look at the roof first?"

She laughed and the sound was like water singing in a brook. "Let me feed you first. Here—you can hold Stevie." She thrust the toddler into his arms.

"But—" Linc clutched the solemn child. They stared at each other, the child looking as bewildered as Linc felt.

"Want me to take her, young fella?" The wizened man spoke between bites. "You seem none too familiar with the breed." He chuckled, and Linc had to smile back.

"I've never held a baby."

"You hang around Ivy long enough, you'll be holding cats, lost puppies and ever' other darn thing she can find to take care of." He shook his head. "That girl—they could run the entire city of Fort Worth off the energy she puts out in a day."

The little girl reached up and grabbed Linc's nose. He recoiled from the pinprick of tiny nails, but tightened his grip so she wouldn't fall.

"Stevie's enamored of you, I see." Ivy was back with a huge slab of pie that had Linc's mouth watering. She set down the plate and glass of tea. Then she smiled at the child and opened her arms. The little girl leaped with a suddenness that took his breath. Ivy cuddled the child. "Sorry about the nails. It's obviously time for a trim."

"No problem," he said. "Your daughter is... cute." He didn't really know what you said about kids.

Ivy's vivid blue eyes darkened. Her shoulders sagged. "She's not my daughter."

A bell rang. "Excuse me, please." Child on her hip, she whirled and headed for the stairs.

Feeling like some kind of heel, though he had no idea why, Linc looked over at the old man, who kept eating. No help from that quarter.

From this vantage point, Linc surveyed the sad state of what had once been a proud old house, this one-story wing now converted into a café. Despite the cleanliness of the place, a lot of work was needed.

Resisting the urge to turn and walk away, he sat

down to try the pie. And when the first bite hit his tongue, Linc couldn't hold back his sigh.

Carl glanced up and grinned. ''Girl sure can cook, can't she?''

Linc nodded, busy chewing. He'd climb Mount Everest for another piece of this.

IVY RAN UP THE STAIRS, shoving back memories. With one hand, she stroked Stevie's back, then pressed a kiss to the dark curls.

She pushed the ache away and turned her thoughts to the man downstairs. Her lips curved upward. If he'd ever had a child in his arms, she'd eat her hat. Still, something in the way that he'd held Stevie—as if she were delicate crystal that might shatter in his hands—tugged at her heart. Behind that awkwardness lay kindness.

His genuine unease when she'd told him Stevie wasn't hers made her feel sorry for him, but the subject of motherhood was not one she discussed. Ever.

Reaching the second floor, Ivy walked through the bedroom door. ''Soup's almost ready, Aunt Prudie. Do you need anything?''

''Nothing that twenty years off my age wouldn't cure. I'm coming downstairs to eat. Can't give that old man the run of the place any longer.''

''Are you sure?'' Ivy bit her tongue. Wasn't that

what she'd been praying for—that her great-aunt would recover? "What am I saying? Of course you're sure."

"What's got you rattled, honey?"

Her great-aunt's eyes were still far too sharp. "Nothing, really."

Aunt Prudie snorted. "You couldn't tell a lie if your life depended on it." She patted the bed beside her. "Come on, sit down. The world won't crumble if you rest for a minute."

Ivy didn't want to rest, but she obeyed. Stevie nestled into her breast, and for one precious moment Ivy felt whole again.

Ten months since—

The thought made her shoot to her feet again. She settled Stevie on the bed and busied herself opening a window, now that the rain had stopped. "Doesn't the world smell wonderful after a rain?"

"Oh, Ivy, sweetheart, are you ever going to give in and cry?"

"Tears aren't the answer," she whispered. Tears wouldn't bring her baby back. Tears wouldn't make her late husband faithful. Another family she'd tried to create was gone, and there weren't enough tears in the world.

The only answer Ivy had ever found was work. She turned with a brittle smile. "I'm glad you want to come downstairs. Everyone's missed you."

Aunt Prudie rolled her eyes. "Don't try to tell me Carl Thompson's sorry I'm not dishing out his portions instead of you. Old man will eat us out of house and home—too stubborn to learn to cook more than bacon and eggs."

Ivy smothered a grin, grateful for the change of topic. Aunt Prudie could complain, but she and Carl didn't let a day go by without each mentioning the other. "Let me take Stevie down and leave her with Carl, then I'll be back to help you—" She saw her great-aunt stiffen. "Just this first time." Ivy leaned down and kissed Aunt Prudie's cheek. "Humor me, all right?"

Aunt Prudie's china-blue eyes sparkled. She cupped Ivy's cheek. "Just as long as you know I could have done it by myself."

"Malone women." Ivy smiled. "I remember Daddy shaking his head, saying there was nothing on this earth more stubborn." She could smile about him now, but she'd always wonder. Was that why he left? Too many hardheaded women in his house?

"And Malone men the most foolish. Imagine my nephew leaving three fine daughters for that floozy."

"She wasn't a floozy, Aunt Prudie. She was a bank vice president."

"Humph. Expensive suit can't hide a woman's

nature. No decent woman would have wanted a man who'd desert a family like that. You had your hands full, and you so young. Oh, Ivy, if only I'd known—''

It had been a terrifying time. Her mother falling apart when her father left. Thirteen-year-old Ivy trying to keep her family together but failing. Three sisters separated: Caroline and Ivy sent to separate foster homes, four-year-old Chloe adopted.

But that was the past. Her parents had been gone for years now.

Stevie wiggled and began babbling, patting Ivy's cheeks. "But you didn't, Auntie. And we survived." Ivy made a face at Stevie, delighting in the little girl's sudden grin. "Come on, Stevie. Let's go see if Carl will play grandpa again."

She went down the stairs more slowly than she'd come up them, hoping the compelling stranger would already be outside.

LINC EMERGED from the storage room where Carl had indicated that he'd find a ladder. It was a ladder in name only, ancient and wooden and rickety, but it would serve his purpose. His ruse had worked. He was one step closer to fulfilling a debt to the brother he should have saved.

He often traveled incognito to examine potential

investments, since his Jaguar and custom suits inevitably drove up prices. He knew a lot about construction—it was how he'd supported himself when he'd been disinherited. Nowadays, though, he paid other people to check out his investments.

Linc wasn't sure what he'd expected after he'd found the to-whom-it-may-concern letters in Garner's office. They'd been only tiny pricks compared with the gaping wound his brother's death had inflicted, a wound made more terrible by the knowledge that any time in the past fifteen years he could have troubled himself to contact, maybe not the father who'd exiled him, but the brother he'd wronged. Instead, he'd hoarded the bitterness of his banishment the way a starving man did his last crust of bread.

If he hadn't, he would have known long ago about the gambling habit that had decimated the family fortune and left them drowning in debt. Had left his brother unable to see any way out but taking his own life.

Linc could have stopped it somehow. Given Garner options, bailed him out.

If only he'd known.

For the others, the loss was six months old; for Linc, two weeks. Had his gravely ill father not been desperate, he would never have relented and sent for his black-sheep son. Linc realized now that his father must have understood all along where to find him.

And hadn't. He'd only sought Linc out for Betsey's sake. Betsey, his brother's widow. The only woman Linc had ever loved.

But there was no easy fix. Even if by some chance his father would accept financial assistance, most of Linc's capital was tied up in a new venture; he could pull none of it yet without risking it all.

The only assets available were land holdings in this town—so inconsequential that Garner had probably forgotten they were here. Once Palo Verde had been the seed corn of the fortune their maternal grandfather, Hartwell, had built. Linc had to use these assets to secure Betsey's financial welfare. It was all he could do for Garner now.

So he was here in dusty, dying Palo Verde, and this woman, who looked nothing at all like the lavender-and-mothballs senior citizen he'd expected, was offering him an opening. A chance at redemption.

As long as he didn't break his neck the first day.

He climbed up on what once had been a two-story house, examining the weathered white paint, the faded blue trim. The roof was dismal. The shingles were probably forty years old if they were a day. The rolling, tree-covered countryside stretching past this town square for miles in each direction caught his gaze, and he stopped and stared.

Shabby like the upholstered arms of an old woman's sofa, Palo Verde lay before him, a tiny village nestled on a carpet of green leaves. The rain had washed it and now it sparkled here and there, like half-scrubbed windows emerging from beneath the dust of time.

Linc's businessman's eyes saw what could amount to thousands and thousands of dollars in needed repairs—an investment on which only pennies would ever be returned. He thought about the woman inside and shook his head. She was lovely and kind, but he had Betsey to care for now. He'd investigate more closely; however, he suspected the best thing to do was to cut Betsey's losses— sell all holdings at fire-sale prices and invest the proceeds in something with a future. He'd already put out some feelers for buyers.

He didn't look forward to telling golden-haired Ivy, though. As he climbed down the ladder, he was so absorbed in casting about for the right words that he didn't notice the cracked rung until it gave way, and he tumbled through the air.

CHAPTER TWO

HALFWAY DOWN THE STAIRS, Ivy heard the ladder bang against the house, then a terrible clatter.

Oh, no. She raced outside, baby in tow, Carl not far behind her.

Linc lay flat on his back, one arm twisted at an odd angle. Still. Too still.

Heart in her throat, she set Stevie on the ground beside her. "Carl, call for help, please. And call Sally to come get the baby." She could hear her voice shaking.

Hands poised above Linc, she tried desperately to remember any first aid she'd ever known. *Don't move him?* Didn't instructions always say don't move the person?

He gasped, his chest expanding with the sudden deep gulp of air. His eyes flew open, his pupils dark and huge. He lifted himself to one arm, groaning.

"What—" He looked at her in confusion.

"Don't sit up," she urged, attempting to ease him back.

At her touch, he flinched. All color drained from his face. He sank back down.

"I'm sorry—" Ivy wanted to help him but was afraid she'd hurt him again. "Can you—?" She leaned closer. "Is it your shoulder?"

He nodded, cradling his right arm with his left hand. The strong bones of his face stood out white against his skin.

"I'm so sorry. Does anything else hurt?" She ran careful fingers over him while she glanced back to gauge his reaction. "Can you move your legs? Oh, please don't—"

He managed to sit up, holding his arm, his broad shoulders hunched against the pain.

"Shouldn't you lie down? Help will be here soon. The nearest emergency room is forty-five miles away in Weatherford, but the ambulance will—"

"I don't need an ambulance." Folding one leg beneath him, he started to rise.

"Are you sure you shouldn't—"

Coming to one knee, he swayed.

Ivy scooted to his good side and slid her arms around his waist. "I wish you'd lie back down," she muttered. "I'm a great cook but a terrible doctor. What if something's irreparably damaged? I warn you, if you sue me, I don't have a cent for you to take."

Linc grunted and leaned into her, feeling the press of her breasts against his left side and wishing his shoulder didn't throb as though someone had stuck a hot poker in it. "I don't want to sue you. I just want to—" He took a step and slipped on the wet grass.

Her slender arms tightened around his waist. Her thighs brushed his as she braced to steady him. The top of her head barely reached his shoulder, and he looked down at the curls escaping in profusion from the pink-and-white flowered fabric imprisoning her long ponytail. When she glanced up at him, worry darkening the blue eyes, Linc was tempted to explain that he wasn't who she thought, that he was a danger to her goals.

Betsey. His duty was to Betsey. But he experienced an unaccustomed streak of fierce protectiveness toward this small, soft, sweet woman.

Carl spared him. "Ivy, they're tied up with an accident on the interstate. It'll be a few—" He stopped as he rounded the corner and saw Linc standing.

"Call back and cancel. I don't need an ambulance." His shoulder hurt like hell and he'd be sore all over tomorrow, but he had played rugby at prep school. He knew what a dislocated shoulder felt like. "I just have to pop this back in place." He forced out the words against the darkness edging into his vision.

"What do you mean?" Ivy whispered.

"He means we can do it ourselves," Carl said.

Ivy tightened her arms around his waist. "Shouldn't we get you to a doctor?"

Linc gritted his teeth. "It can't wait. It will swell too much." He glanced over at the old man. "Will you help me?"

He could tell the old man knew how it felt.

Carl nodded. "Ivy girl, you'll have to help hold him down."

Her eyes widened. "Why does he have to be held down?"

"You'll have to keep his shoulder in place while I pull on his arm. He'll likely pass out, so let's get him somewhere that he can stay awhile."

Ivy looked horrified. She glanced back at Linc, studying his face.

"I'll make it." Linc clenched his jaw. "Let's get it done."

Then the woman who juggled babies and old men and pies stepped to the forefront. "All right." She nodded. "Can you climb the stairs? I've been redoing the rooms for a bed-and-breakfast, and one of them has a bed."

"Floor's better." He bit out each word. "Won't sag."

Carl nodded. "Got to keep the ball and socket lined up, Ivy. Can't risk pinching nerves in that shoulder."

She peered behind Linc. "Then, let's take him to my cottage in back. He won't have to climb stairs, and the floor is carpeted if he winds up lying there for a while." She looked up at him. "Can you walk that far?"

Linc nodded, not even checking to see how far it was. He'd do what needed doing. "Let's go."

"Just a minute," she said, leaning down to scoop up Stevie.

She gazed at Linc, perfectly composed now, soothing him as though he were a child himself. "You're going to be fine. I'll watch over you."

Even through the sharp pain, Linc wanted to grin. The old man was right. She took on every lost cause in her path.

Like a ragtag small-town parade, the odd procession moved toward the little white cottage nestled in the trees behind the diner.

THANK GOODNESS, Sally only lived two blocks away. She'd picked up her baby, blanched at the sight of Linc's shoulder and left in a hurry after promising to check on Aunt Prudie and take the pies out of the oven.

Ivy studied the man stretched out on the worn Turkish rug of her living room, his eyes closed, face white and pinched beneath his tan.

"Are you sure about this?"

Pain-filled gray eyes opened. "I've done this before. It will be better afterward."

Ivy turned to Carl for confirmation. Carl looked grim. "We didn't used to worry about docs for this sort of thing, Ivy. Out working cattle, you just popped the shoulder back in and hunkered down for a few days. It'll be all right, you'll see.''

She drew a deep breath. "All right. Tell me what to do.''

Carl cocked his head and addressed Linc. "There's too much difference in your sizes. She won't be able to hold you down.'' He rubbed one finger over his chin. "How about you sit up on this straight-backed chair and she stands behind you? That way I can work from below with some clearance, and the chair will brace you. She can wrap one arm across your chest and one from behind, like this—''

He demonstrated on Ivy. "Can you do that, Ivy girl?''

Her stomach rolled at the thought of hurting Linc, but he was already in a lot of pain. There was nowhere to go but forward. She would strive to be as controlled as Linc. "I can do it.''

"Take his shirt off first, so I can see what I'm doing.''

Keeping her hands gentle, she complied, trying not to stare at the broad expanse of bare skin. Then one more time they moved him. He sat in the chair from her kitchen table, his head at her chin level. Ivy stood behind him, leaning over the back of the chair and laying her arm across his chest. The movement brought her cheek against his hair, and she was surprised at its softness. It was raven'swing black, with curl that fought the short cut probably intended to tame it.

"You ready, girl?" Carl asked. "I'm going to pull his arm out and down. Brace his chest and don't let me move his body forward or we'll prolong his pain needlessly."

Ivy searched for a handhold, and finally gripped one belt loop of his jeans with each hand, digging her heels into the floor. "Ready."

She wanted to close her eyes but didn't dare. As Carl pulled Linc's arm out at a sickening angle, Ivy felt Linc stiffen, saw beads of sweat pop out on his skin, but he never uttered a sound. She held on tight, praying this would be over soon.

A *pop* sounded. Carl let go, and Linc slumped against the back of the chair, closing his eyes.

Ivy held her breath. "Is it over?" she whispered. She still clasped Linc, one hand now sliding up and down his side to soothe him as she would soothe Stevie.

"It's over." Carl nodded. "Let's get him to lie down. Help me move him."

"I can do it," the deep voice answered.

He stirred. Only now noticing she was stroking him, she dropped her arms and stepped away.

"You got anything we can bind that arm to his side with, Ivy? Elastic bandages? Long strips of fabric?"

"I'll find something." Cheeks burning, Ivy jumped up and ran to her linen closet. For a moment she just stood there, staring at the linens as though they were foreign objects.

She pressed one hand to her fluttering stomach, then pulled out an old sheet. With her sewing scissors, she began cuts for strips as she walked. Tearing off one long strip, she returned to the living room.

"Here," she said. "Start with this. I'll cut more."

"You let me cut. I suspect you'd wrap this better than I would with these old arthritic hands."

"What do I do?"

"Just bind his arm to his side. Got to give those ligaments and tendons time to tighten back in the right place. And we need to ice the shoulder for a while."

Ivy knelt by the chair, and Linc sat up straight, holding his left arm out from his body. Gnawing on her lower lip, she concentrated on wrapping his chest as if he were a mummy.

That chest was a problem. Naked. Broad.

Touching his skin made her feel…strange. Uneasy and too warm and…edgy.

Linc stared straight ahead. Ivy leaned across him, then rocked back, across and back again, each time brushing his chest as she struggled to reach around him. Each time trying to ignore the feel of him, each time failing.

And every touch stung Linc. Her unruly golden curls slid like silk across his throat and chin, her soft breasts skimmed his chest. Though his shoulder still ached like the very devil, the searing pain was gone, leaving him only too aware of the woman whose even white teeth nipped at a full lower lip that was going to drive him crazy if she didn't move away soon.

And she still smelled of cinnamon and flowers.

Finally, she finished. His upper arm was immobilized against his body. She fashioned a sling from the fabric that was left and fastened it gently around his lower arm for support.

Then she settled back on her heels. "There." Her color had returned, her face now flushed with the exertion. Uncertain blue eyes lifted to his. "How do you feel?"

"Fine."

"I doubt that." Then the blue eyes filled with tears. "I am so sorry," she whispered. "This is my fault."

He looked down at her, struck by an incomprehensible urge to murmur comforting words and press a tender kiss to her forehead.

He was not a tender man, never had been. And she was so far from his type it was laughable. Instead, he fisted his unencumbered hand on his thigh. First the pain and now the wane in adrenaline were making him light-headed. "Forget it."

But she was too sensitive not to notice. She glanced around her, then at Carl. "He's too tall for my sofa. Help me get him to my bed, Carl."

"I'll be fine." Linc gripped the back of the chair. "I can walk. I need to leave now." He shoved to his feet, then swayed.

Lightning-fast, she was under his good arm, supporting him. "You're not going anywhere but bed. This way—before you pass out." Her voice no longer sounded stricken. Speaking was the major-domo who had overseen pies and old men and children.

"I don't pass out." Dots swam before his eyes.

She kept one arm clamped to his waist, the other on the hand slung over her shoulder. She would be crushed if he fell.

Linc concentrated on not falling. The cottage was tiny, and just about the time his head began to clear, they'd made it inside her bedroom. He sank gratefully to the quilt that covered the bed, vaguely noting that the room smelled like her.

"Just for a minute," he mumbled. He felt her remove his shoes, heard their voices as if from a distance as they shifted him until he could stretch out.

He tried to open his eyes, thinking that he needed to head back to Dallas or at least call his assistant and check for messages.

But delicate hands arranged a pillow beneath his head and stroked his hair. Before he could do anything he should do...Linc slid into slumber.

IVY JUMPED UP at the first groan. Slipping a robe over her nightgown, she left the sofa and headed for her bedroom.

He'd twisted off all the covers, and moonlight spread silver fingers over his exposed body. When he'd still been sound asleep at eleven, she'd removed his pants and socks with the quick, impartial hands of a nurse, but it had felt like an invasion of this reserved man's privacy.

It felt that way again, but Ivy was having a hard time not looking.

He was lean—too lean, really. He needed some fattening up. Judging from the looks of his pickup and the age of his jeans, he might have fallen on hard times.

And now he was injured and probably couldn't afford a doctor. He didn't like asking for help, but surely he'd see that she owed him. The least she could do was take care of him for a few days and feed him up, so that when he left, he'd be well rested and strong.

Not that he didn't look plenty strong as he lay there. He might be lean, but he was all muscle, his broad chest dusted with dark hair tapering to a fine line below the bandage and drifting down inside—

Part of him stirred, and Ivy jerked her gaze upward.

His eyes were open.

"Oh—I'm sorry, I—" She glanced anywhere but at his body. "How are you feeling?"

Linc lay there, naked but for briefs and a bandage, and stared at the vision she made, hair tumbling, eyes huge and aware. A thin white robe sprinkled with flowers topped a simple white cotton gown.

She should look virginal and plain and boring.

Too bad his body didn't agree. She was the most feminine thing he'd ever set eyes on. Delicate and curvy, she was the very definition of *woman*.

He jerked his gaze away. "What time is it?"

"About three. Would you like some aspirin? I'm afraid that's all I have." She'd moved at last, crossing to the bed and feeling his forehead.

Her fingers were cool respite. He wanted to press his face into them. Let himself sink into the comfort Ivy exuded as naturally as breath.

"It aches, but I don't need anything. Except—" He shot a glance toward the bathroom.

"Oh—" He could hear the blush. Then her voice turned businesslike and neutral. "Of course. Would you like some help?"

Linc chuckled. "I think I can do that myself."

She withdrew, pulling her robe together. But she returned his smile. "I meant help getting up."

"No." With so little on, the last thing he needed was to have her touch him.

Linc rolled to his left side and shoved himself to sitting. Ivy backed toward the door. He started to stand, but having one arm bound affected his balance.

She was at his side in an instant, steadying him.

Linc tightened his arm around her, yielding this time to a sudden insane desire to touch her.

She went as still as stone in his embrace. Her head drifted back, the honey curls spilling over his arm. Her eyes were as dark as midnight, her lips slightly parted, her chest rising on a ragged inhalation.

Then her unfocused expression gave way to shock…shadowed with something that looked too much like fear. "I—will you be all right now? I— I'd better—I'll get more ice." She stepped out of his grip, moved back one step, hands fisting in her robe.

Linc gathered an uneven breath and cursed himself roundly. He didn't understand the effect she had on him. Again he acknowledged that she was all wrong. She was puppies and kittens and white picket fences. Babies and lifelong commitments.

His type was independent, tough women who knew what they wanted and had lives of their own that didn't involve too much of his time. He never even spent the night with any of them after sex. He preferred to sleep alone.

So why did this woman stir him so? She was the most innocent person he'd ever met over the age of consent, far too tender and vulnerable for someone like him. He was here for Betsey, and he would inevitably cause Ivy sorrow. He had no right to make things worse, no matter what she stirred in him.

He wasn't a sentimental man, but he'd never considered himself cruel, either. He was logical and practical and businesslike. He made decisions based on the facts, not emotion.

His voice rough, he simply nodded and didn't look at her again as he said, ''I'm fine. I'll be leaving at first light.''

CHAPTER THREE

WHEN FIRST LIGHT CAME, though, it was Ivy who crept around her cottage and readied herself for the day. She had always been an early riser, so not having an alarm clock by the sofa didn't matter. She hadn't slept after the encounter, anyway.

She'd listened to him move around in the moonlight, then heard him sink into the bed again with a groan. She'd wanted to go check on him, but something deep within uttered a warning.

This man was dangerous. Sorrow hovered in his eyes. His quiet strength called to her.

With a great sigh of relief, Ivy opened up the back door to the diner. She turned on the lights, headed for the washer and started a load that included his clothes. She'd have them back before he even awakened. It was the least she could do.

She switched on the coffeepot she'd readied last night, tiptoed up the stairs to check on Aunt Prudie, then came back down and began preparations for the breakfast run. As she mixed and kneaded the dough for the much-requested cinnamon coffee cake, which had become a staple on the menu, Ivy looked across the street at the darkened windows of the stone courthouse, the ungainly, once-beautiful buildings that lined the square.

A hundred fifty years ago, pioneers had carved Palo Verde from wilderness into a thriving center built on cattle and cedar; in recent years, too many of Palo Verde's sons and daughters had fled to the cities, abandoning it to the same fate as many small towns.

She had ideas to change that. One day there would be more than the handful of tourists who wandered in off the highway from Mineral Wells. Just yesterday, she'd had a couple stop by who said they'd heard about the diner from friends in Fort Worth. They'd left singing her praises. Ivy felt a stirring of pride…and hope. If everyone would hang together and if the absentee landlord would just understand that all they needed was a little help and a chance—

It could work. This little town had only gone to sleep like Rip van Winkle, not died as everyone said. Its rich history was still here, and the people were good as gold.

Palo Verde deserved better than to be forgotten, swept under the rug. She hadn't been able to stop her father from leaving or her husband from cheating or drinking and driving. She hadn't been able to keep from losing the precious baby once nestled inside her. But these people who had welcomed her into their hearts in the darkest months of her life were stirring to hope, and she could not, *would not,* let that hope die.

Right then, Ivy made up her mind that she'd write one more letter. She punched down the rising dough for her cinnamon coffee cake, hard.

If the company didn't answer her in a week, she would take the unprecedented step of closing the diner for a day and heading for Dallas to beard the lion in his den.

If only she could figure out who the lion was.

She would not let Linc's presence distract her. She had too much else to do, and he'd be gone soon enough, anyway. He was attractive—so what? Her husband had been good-looking, and she'd let that blind her to his nature. Her friends had tried to warn her, and she hadn't listened. Yes, Linc looked as though he needed a friend, but Jimmy had needed her, too—yet her love hadn't been enough to keep him home. He'd been with a girlfriend the night he drove drunk and crashed the car. The pregnant Ivy had quit being a naive fool that night. In the midst of her grief and shock, she had lost the last precious piece of her lifelong dream to have a family of her own.

As memory cracked the careful casing around

her heart, Ivy began kneading the dough as though she could squeeze out the agony trapped inside her.

Drawing a deep, slow breath, she concentrated as she had taught herself. *This one moment.* Just walk through it, one step at a time.

And don't mistake need for love ever again.

LINC FINALLY SWAM UP through the dark waters of a troubled sleep. The scent of fresh coffee teased him awake. He turned to locate it. Pain yanked his eyes wide-open.

His shoulder. The bandage. The fall crowded back.

"Good morning," Ivy said from the doorway. "You were stirring, so I thought you might like coffee."

The incredible scent hit him once more. Glancing over at the bedside table, he saw a steaming mug.

"Wha—" He cleared his throat and tried again. "What time is it?" He straightened an arm to lever himself up, wincing.

"Here, let me help you." She crossed to him, then leaned over, bracing his back while slipping pillows behind him. The unique fragrance of her revived an image…golden hair loose and spilling over her shoulders.

His body responded. He jerked away.

Ivy stepped back, color rising, fingers tangling. "How do you feel?" She glanced at him, then away.

"Fine," he snapped.

"I'm sorry. It's early and I—" Her eyes looked everywhere but at him. "I have to get back. Saturday's not as busy as other mornings, not this early, but—"

"Stop." He held up one hand. "Give me a minute. I'm not good before my second cup of coffee."

"Oh." Her shoulders eased. "One of those. Like my husband."

He stopped with the cup halfway to his mouth. "You're married?"

"Was," she corrected him. "I'm a widow." A faint laugh escaped her, but he heard no humor in it. "Or something."

"What does that mean?"

"Nothing." She shook her head and busied herself straightening his covers. "It's not important."

Her hands smoothed the sheet too close to a body fully aware of her. There was an innocence about her that made him too conscious of being all but naked. He needed to get her out of here. "So who's minding the store?"

She checked the clock.

"Oh, mercy—is there anything you need before I go?"

He shook his head.

"I can bring you breakfast later."

"I'll come over to the café."

"Maybe you should stay in bed."

He lifted one eyebrow. "You want to join me?"

She gasped. "No, of course not. I—" Deep color stained her cheeks. "Of course not. I have to go now. Come—" Her voice faltered. Drawing herself up straight, she walked to the doorway. "Come whenever you're ready."

"Ivy—" His apology arrived too late. He heard the front door close. Carefully, though he'd earned a hard slam.

He'd make that apology. His turmoil was not her fault.

Sipping coffee that was as amazing as her pie, Linc glanced around the room. Tiny, but spotless and neat. White wallpaper dotted with violets, sheer white curtains over the windows, a lacy white bedspread topped with an ancient quilt faded to pastels. The room was as feminine as the woman who slept here.

Why wasn't she the cranky blue hair he'd imagined the letter writer to be?

His spirits soared. The real Ivy was far too real to him already, and far too intriguing. Betsey's future welfare depended upon his making a sound business decision based on logic and reason.

Ivy's allure could not supersede his reason for being here. His inexplicable attraction to her was a problem, but he'd made a career of problem-solving. He'd just have to be wary, most of all with Ivy. She was too soft, too tender. He wouldn't like himself much if he hurt her. So rule number one was to keep his body under control.

Rule number two would be to take advantage of the opportunity to observe Ivy's crusade up close. Perhaps, though it wasn't really his concern, there was a way to turn her attention to something more productive. He'd study the situation the way he'd study a company's financials. Figure out, as he did when acquiring new investments, where Ivy's strengths and weaknesses lay, what she wanted that he could supply in exchange for her relinquishing her half-baked idea.

Perhaps, if the rest of her food measured up to the example set by her pie and coffee, he'd offer to set her up in a more suitable location, one where she could hire proper help and merely supervise. Stop working so hard for so little reward.

There. He felt better. He had the beginnings of a plan. Without a plan, goals could never be achieved. Without sufficient research, a good plan was unlikely.

Linc finished off the coffee and edged out of bed. He spotted his clothes lying in an old white rocking chair, neatly folded. When he touched them, he could discern a trace of warmth from the dryer.

Damn. She'd washed his clothes and brought him coffee.

She'd stroked his hair in the night. Given him her bed.

He could still feel the curves of her body, see her in the doorway, moonlight on a gown so modest it shouldn't have heated his blood.

Ivy Parker stood in the way of a promise. Something deep within him told him that she was dangerous in a way he didn't yet understand. He didn't like that.

He shook his head, refusing to let fancy sway him. He took his clean clothes into the bathroom and started unwinding the bandage from a body that could still feel her touch.

He had a mission, damn it. She would not upset it.

IVY HAD JUST PULLED more biscuits from the oven, and was reaching for the bacon, when the back of her neck prickled.

She turned, and there Linc stood, big and too real.

Her heart raced as though it belonged to a green girl. She didn't like it, not a bit.

He'd removed the makeshift wrappings, though he'd replaced the sling. His midnight hair sparkled with drops of moisture.

He caught her look. "Thanks for the shower."

Ivy didn't want to think about Linc in her shower.

Naked.

She shifted back to the griddle and laid out strips of bacon. "You're welcome." She concentrated on her cooking.

"Ivy, listen, I was out of line back there—"

"Are you hungry?" She picked up her spatula, still not looking at him.

He hesitated, frowning.

"Do you like hash browns? Your body will need fuel to heal."

"Ivy—" With one finger, he turned her head toward him.

"How many eggs do you want?"

For a long moment, their gazes locked, his impenetrable beneath those dark, forbidding brows.

A muscle jumped in his jaw. "Three would be good."

She cracked the shells. "How do you like them?"

"You don't have to go to any more trouble for me."

"No trouble. How do you want them?"

He sighed. "Over easy."

"Fine." She stared at the griddle and not at him. With practiced ease, she flipped the eggs, scooped them onto a plate, added hash browns, bacon and two biscuits, then moved toward him. "Go ahead and sit down. I'll carry this for you. Want more coffee?"

"I can handle it." He stood in her way, scowling. "I didn't thank you yet. For the coffee. For…everything."

She shrugged. "It's nothing." She held on to the plate, wishing he'd move away.

"You washed my clothes." He made it sound like an accusation.

She lifted one eyebrow, holding the plate between them. Temper stirred. "You'd rather wear them dirty?"

"No, I—" He blew out a breath. He seemed as unsettled as she felt. "Look, Ivy, you don't owe me anything. I fell. It was an accident. You didn't make it happen."

She was steaming now, and she couldn't have explained why if her life had depended upon it. He just made her feel edgy. Threatened. Angry that she cared. "Why did you remove the bandage? Carl said a few days."

The dark brows snapped together again. "I'm not a child—or a lost soul. It's not the first time I've done this. I know how to take care of myself."

"Fine." She shoved the plate at him. "Then, go eat. I'm busy. I have customers waiting."

"I'm paying for this breakfast. Got that?" He took the plate in his one good hand and stomped away.

"Over my dead body," she muttered.

Aunt Prudie and Mabel, the diner's veteran waitress, were staring at her from the counter, mouths hanging open, when she turned.

"What are you staring at?"

Aunt Prudie's eyes crinkled. Mabel looked bewildered.

"So *he's* what's got you so rattled." Aunt Prudie grinned. "About time somebody did." She faced her longtime friend. "Better get that boy some silverware and some coffee, Mabel. Ivy and I—we need to have us a little chat."

"Uh-uh," Mabel said. "You say one word while I'm gone and you're gonna have to repeat it." She peered at Ivy. "What's got into you, girl? We thought you were born without the temper gene." She grinned and shook her head. "Nothing like a good-lookin' man to get a woman's dander up.'' She finished pouring the coffee and headed off toward Linc's table, humming.

"Oh, golly," Ivy whispered, her head sinking into her hands. "What in heaven's name am I doing?"

Aunt Prudie reached out toward her from her perch on a tall stool and patted Ivy's shoulder. "It's all right, honey. Any woman would be thrown off balance by a handsome rascal like that. But those are the most fun."

"I don't want fun. I don't even know him, Aunt Prudie. And I don't need a man in my life."

Aunt Prudie chuckled. "From the look on that man's face, I don't think he's too happy about it, either. But Ivy, honey, the heart wants what it wants. Nothing you can do about that."

"You just watch," Ivy muttered, and resumed her place at the griddle.

So THERE WAS FIRE beneath the sweetness, Linc thought.

Damn. A saint could be set on a pedestal and admired from a distance. She'd seemed so soft and harmless, a delicate angel too good to be true.

Hell. Right now that delicate angel looked as though she'd just as soon drive one of those knives through his heart.

A full mug of coffee appeared by his plate, followed by silverware wrapped in a napkin. Linc glanced up to see a large woman, rough around the edges but with kind brown eyes. She was grinning from ear to ear.

She held out a hand, chuckling. "I'm Mabel Dixon, and I'd like to shake your hand."

Linc had to use his left hand. "Why is that?"

"'Cause nobody around here knew Ivy had a temper. Kinda reassuring to find out the girl's human. What did you do?"

"I'm not quite sure," he admitted.

Mabel laughed. "You really sleep in her bed last night?"

Linc frowned. Word certainly got around. "She wasn't in it. Don't assume—"

Mabel waved off his objections. "Get on with you. What goes on in the night isn't anyone's business. But our sweet Ivy seems rattled. She avoids eligible men like the plague. I told her she couldn't stay in cold storage forever. Too much heart in that girl to give it all to old folks and babies." She nodded at his plate. "Best eat that before it gets cold. Ivy's biscuits are a slice of pure sin. I'll be by with more coffee soon." Giving him an outrageous wink, she walked away.

Great. Any hope of anonymity had firmly fled. Half the eyes in this place were looking his way.

So Ivy was rattled, too. Mabel was right. It

wasn't just anger he'd seen in her eyes. And why did she avoid men—she, who seemed the perfect candidate for marriage and babies? What was the story on the dead husband?

The butter had melted on the biscuits. Linc took one bite of the mouthwatering treat and sighed. Slice of pure sin was right.

Ivy was turning out to be a complex woman, and he didn't need the distraction. If he had an ounce of sense, he would go home as soon as he finished eating. Put his lawyer on the case first thing Monday. Negotiate from a distance.

But understanding Ivy would give him the information to make the best decision for Betsey. Ivy was the one who'd written the letters, after all. She was the crusader. He didn't think she'd stop until she got an answer.

Therefore, he should stay and figure her out. It was simple logic—nothing personal. Strictly business. He'd solve the puzzle of Ivy Parker. It wouldn't take long once he applied his full attention to it. He could keep his hands to himself. He was in control, as always.

Everything figured out and neatly organized, Linc settled in to enjoy one of the best meals of his life.

CHAPTER FOUR

LINC STOOD in Ivy's bedroom after breakfast, frowning at the strips of bandage. The sling wasn't enough, and he'd known it even when he'd barked at Ivy; he just hated asking for help. But every movement set fire to the grinding ache in his shoulder. It should be wrapped again, if only he could figure out how to do it one handed. Thank goodness he was left-handed, but that wasn't enough.

He wondered if Carl would show up at the diner today. Ivy was busy, even if he wanted to ask her for help. Which he didn't. Not with the memory of her full breasts brushing over his chest.

He threw down the bandages. Maybe he'd go to his truck and retrieve his cell phone. Call the office and see what was cooking. The Sampson deal needed attention. That tract in Phoenix would be prime commercial land within a decade.

That was it. Work was his dependable friend. He'd check in with his assistant first—

Then he remembered. It was Sunday. His office was closed.

Damn Sundays, anyway. Weekends, holidays— so much time wasted. His schedule didn't recognize them. That others did was an inconvenience. He'd long ago learned to use the quiet time to formulate strategies, make plans. Do the big-picture thinking, as well as stay ahead of the competition by going the extra mile.

He could call his assistant, Maggie, at home; it wouldn't be the first time. But Maggie, at the age of fifty-six, had recently acquired a love interest, and Linc's genuine fondness for the woman who was his most trusted colleague made him hesitate to interrupt whatever plans she might have.

Still, idleness had never sat well with Linc, not since the wake-up call that ended his wild, reckless youth. Dead broke when he'd started out, he'd gotten where he was by dint of endless hours of back-breaking construction work during the day, then going to school at night. Weekends had been a luxury he couldn't afford.

That hard work had created a good life for him in Denver. He wanted that life back. He wanted to figure out what to do with these buildings in Palo Verde quickly, take care of his obligations to the past, then return as soon as possible to his own world.

First things first. Linc picked up the bandages and started again.

"Here, let me help you with that."

At the sound of Ivy's voice, Linc whirled, jarring his injured shoulder. The bandage slipped, and he swore.

"Hold still," Ivy said, catching the crumpled length before it hit the floor.

"I don't need your help."

"You do, but you wish you didn't." Keeping her gaze fastened on the strips of cloth, she secured his arm to his side, leaning closer each time she transferred the bandage from one hand to another.

"You shouldn't be leaving today. You should rest."

He ground his teeth. "I've been taking care of myself for a long time now."

"Everyone needs help sometimes."

He cocked one eyebrow. "I don't see you taking any."

She didn't look up. "I take what I need. Lift up your arm."

Linc held himself very still, left arm out at an angle, and tried to ignore the warmth exuding from her body, the bread scent that clung to her hair. When her breasts grazed his chest, his breath escaped in a hiss.

Ivy forced her gaze up and saw his jaw clenched, his eyes dark and—

Hot. Shadowed by thick dark lashes that did nothing to shield the power of that gaze.

Ivy dropped her eyes to the bandages. "I—I'm almost finished—" Her fingers fumbled as she tried to tuck in the end of a bandage, and her fingers brushed the ridges of muscle just above his navel—

He sucked in another breath. So did she. She jerked away, then grasped at the loose end before everything unraveled.

"Forget it. I'll finish," he barked.

"Just let me—" She tried a second time to tuck in the end, but her fingers wouldn't obey her.

He grabbed her hand, his voice tight. "Damn it, Ivy—" Linc wrested the end of the bandage from her. "Leave it alone."

Cheeks on fire and heart pounding, Ivy couldn't look up. Couldn't face him. "I didn't—I was just—"

Mortified at what had gone through her mind for a dangerous second, Ivy did the only thing she could think to do—

She fled.

Linc didn't turn around to watch. He didn't dare. His life had been disrupted; that was all. He wasn't really attracted to her. It was only that he was grieving for his brother, unsettled by dealing with his father again after all these years. Uneasy trying to sort out his feelings about Betsey. Ivy exuded warmth and comfort. She spoke to something in him long buried.

But she was still the crank letter writer who wanted foolish things he could never give. No sane businessman would bow to her requests, even with extenuating circumstances. He hadn't made a fortune by being foolish; he didn't yield to impulse, not anymore. Time and hard knocks had cured his reckless streak. He was a man of control and caution now, his hot blood gone cool and still.

He was tired—that was it—and his shoulder ached like hell. But he was close to blowing the opportunity that had presented itself. Ivy felt obligated to him; if he asked, she'd let him stay. He'd trade her work for room and board for a few days while he figured out this place. He and Ivy had different goals, but there was a way to compromise; he needed facts to structure that compromise, facts he couldn't get long-distance.

But first, he had some fence mending to do. As red as Ivy's cheeks had been when she fled, an invitation to stay wouldn't be forthcoming just yet. She'd be eager to see him go, no matter how she was tempted, too.

The thought unearthed a smile. *Yes, Ivy Parker. You may be a scold and you may have impractical goals, but somewhere inside, you want me as badly as a foolish part of me wants you.*

But acting on that wanting would be a stupid move, and Lincoln Galloway III was not a stupid man.

IVY JERKED OPEN the screen door at the back of the café, then stubbed her toe racing over the last step. Doubled over by the stabbing pain, she wanted to cry. Wanted to scream.

She would do neither. He didn't deserve tears she'd shed for no one else. "He's only a man," she muttered.

"Oh, but hon—" Mabel appeared in the kitchen, letting out a long wolf whistle. "What a man."

Ivy jumped at the sound of Mabel's voice. "Stop spying on me," she ordered.

"I'm not spying." Mabel indicated the dishes in her hands. "I'm bussing tables." She set them by the sink. "Late-morning travelers."

"I thought everyone had cleared out except the coffee crowd," Ivy said, remorse rushing over her. "I wouldn't have left if—"

"I can make eggs and toast in a pinch, sugar. You know that." Mabel peered at her. "But I want to get back to Linc. Mmm, mmm. That's some kind of man."

Ivy turned away, briskly donned a clean apron and shrugged. "If that's your taste."

Mabel's laugh had always been hearty, suggesting a woman who'd seen the back end of fifty but who'd had a lot of fun over the years. "Oh, darlin'," she chided. "That man would suit any woman's taste 'less she's dead."

Ivy busied herself measuring flour for biscuits and said nothing.

"You've done a good job of playing possum, hon, but I don't think you're dead just yet," Mabel went on. "Blind, either."

Ivy didn't answer.

Mabel's voice softened. "What is it, Ivy girl?" She placed one hand on Ivy's back. "Look, I know that boy got under your skin, but is it really such a terrible thing? Seems to me you deserve something for yourself. You've been stretching yourself real thin for six months now, taking care of Prudie and Carl and Sally's baby, running this place, which is no cakewalk, and writing letters to that hotshot in Dallas. I know you've got this idea about making Palo Verde interesting to tourists, but when does Ivy get her turn?"

Ivy felt Mabel's hand stroke down her back, and for a treacherous second, unshed tears burned. "I don't need a turn." Though she was afraid of what might show on her face, still she looked at the older woman and grasped her free hand. "I appreciate it—really I do. I know you worry about me, but you shouldn't."

Carefully, she measured salt with unsteady hands. "I'm fine, Mabel. I don't need anything. I like what I'm doing."

She stiffened against the press of Mabel's sympathy. If she ever started crying, she'd never stop.

Finally, thank God, Mabel turned away, though not before Ivy saw in her eyes that the older woman wasn't convinced. That didn't matter. All that mattered was staying busy, staying productive.

Mabel stopped a pace away. "Just so you know that there are people who care about you, hon. You're not alone, not anymore."

"Thank you, Mabel," Ivy whispered, then cleared her throat. "Would you change the chalkboard, please? The special will be fried chicken with all the trimmings."

Mabel hesitated for just a moment. "You know I've got good ears for listening, don't you, Ivy?"

Ivy swallowed hard. "I know. I swear I do." She lifted eyes gone hazy. "Thanks, Mabel."

The older woman nodded and left the kitchen, just as Carl walked in.

LINC APPROACHED the back door of the café and paused before knocking. Through the screen door,

he heard Carl's voice first, then Ivy's. He hesitated
with his hand inches from the wood, not sure if it
would be better to have Carl as a buffer or to wait
until Ivy was alone.

Then the next words caught his attention.

"That no-'count, low-life SOB don't care about
your letters, Ivy. Don't you get it?"

"I can make him see, if I can just get him to
talk to me, Carl."

"How do you propose to do that? You ain't
even got a name to go on, just some faceless corporation."

"I'm going to Dallas."

Linc's brows rose.

"I'm going to write one more letter, and if in a
week there's no answer, I'm closing the café for a
day and I'm going to Dallas. Once I find him, I'll
camp out in his office until he agrees to see me.
I'm not going to let these people down, Carl."

Oh boy. Linc's mind raced. Ivy might be unso-
phisticated about how to search for information,
but what she lacked in guile, she more than made
up for in determination. A visit to the Dallas Public
Library would soon speed her on her way.

But when she got to the corporation's location,
she would discover no one there. To save for Betsey what little capital was left, he'd dismissed his
father's staff, giving them severance pay from his

own pocket. Ivy would encounter darkened offices and nothing more.

He glanced around the shabby surroundings Ivy kept so meticulously clean and wondered what the loss of a day's receipts would do to her. He had to stop her from making that trip, but how to do that without revealing his identity?

Just tell her who you are, that there's no chance the landlord will help out, and be done with it. Move on.

If he did that, though, she wouldn't forgive his deception; somehow he was sure of that. He might not know nearly enough about Ivy Parker, but he already understood that she'd been hurt. He had no wish to hurt her more.

Yes, he desired her, unsuited as they were. But more than that, he admired her. Admired her compassion and her—

Spunk.

That was it. Ivy Parker had spunk. Here, in this place the world had passed by, where you could feel the breath of the past on your skin, Ivy resembled nothing so much as the women who must have worked beside their men to build this place. Pioneer women, who'd come to a harsh land and left everything familiar behind. Women who'd nurtured the future as Ivy was nurturing this town's faint hope to stave off the death that took so many small towns.

She might be a hopeless romantic about Palo Verde's potential, but he found himself unwilling to crush that hope.

If she went to Dallas, that hope would die a fast death. He could see no choice but to continue his subterfuge until he could offer Ivy something to make up for what she couldn't have. But he'd better come up with it quick.

The first step was to secure her invitation to stay.

Linc's hand moved forward; he knocked.

At the sound, Ivy turned, expecting the frozen-food deliveryman. When she saw the tall frame filling the doorway, she cast Linc a glance and spun away. "Come in." She kept careful politeness in her tone. "May I help you with something?"

Out of the corner of her eye, she saw Carl's face light up.

"How's the shoulder, Linc?" he asked.

Ivy finished mixing the biscuit dough and began to knead, never looking up.

"Not bad." The rumble of his voice rippled down her spine.

Ivy concentrated harder on the dough, trying to forget what a fool she'd made of herself. You'd think she'd never seen a naked chest before.

Well, all right, she hadn't seen one like *that*. Not up close, anyway.

Bless Carl for being a talkative soul when she couldn't think of one word to say.

"You headin' out today, Ivy says."

"No. I'm not."

Ivy froze.

Linc continued. "This shoulder won't bother me long, and I've still got one good arm. Looks to me like there's plenty of work to be done around here." Ivy could hear his voice directed toward her, and she knew she had to respond.

If she didn't stop soon, the biscuit dough would be tough beyond saving. "I told you I can't afford to pay you."

"We could make a trade," Linc said.

Ivy's throat didn't seem to want to work.

"Maybe room and board in exchange for labor." His voice held an odd note she couldn't decipher.

Silence expanded to fill the room. Carl was staring at her, but she couldn't come up with an explanation that didn't involve either embarrassment or digging into a past she had no intention of discussing.

"Ivy?" Carl said.

She was being rude to a man whose pride had

already taken a beating, judging from the condition of his clothes and truck. There was no excuse for that, and heaven knows she could use the help.

"Never mind," Linc said, and she could hear him moving away.

"Wait—" Hands sticky with dough, she faced him.

Unease flickered in his eyes as if he were no more comfortable than she was about what had passed between them. About needing to ask for help.

Ivy swallowed hard and began wiping her hands on a towel. "That would be…nice." She unbent. "Actually, it would be a godsend, if you're sure you can spare the time." She could keep her hands to herself, and meanwhile, she couldn't afford to turn down free help.

He shrugged. "I've got a few days. And I might be getting the better end of the deal, based on the food I've had so far." Then he smiled, and that smile transformed his rugged features. The smile was deadly, all the more so because she was sure he didn't smile often.

Relief was on his face, too, and Ivy was ashamed that she'd hesitated so long. It wasn't like her to ignore someone in need, and that was what he was at heart: a man down on his luck who could use a break. That he could provide some help she sorely needed was a bonus.

"You won't be working today, though, or using that arm until your shoulder is well," she said.

Linc frowned, and Carl chuckled.

"She's a bossy thing, but her heart's in the right place," Carl said. "And you ain't lived until you've had her chocolate cake."

Warning shaded Linc's voice as a different man looked at her. "Thank you, Dr. Parker, but I've been grown a long time now. I know when I'm well enough to work. The shoulder is nothing."

The message was clear. This man might be down on his luck, but he wasn't a charity case—and he didn't need a mother.

Displeasure would be good for keeping her thoughts in line. Ivy returned to her biscuits. "Fine. After the lunch run, we can make a list."

"I like this," Carl chortled. "Ivy is sweet, sure enough, but she could use someone to keep her in line."

"You mind your own business, Carl Thompson," Ivy said, slapping the dough on the marble and grabbing her rolling pin.

Carl only laughed harder. "Come on, boy," he said, clapping a hand on Linc's good shoulder. "Nice to have a man around after all these women."

"You want chocolate cake in the next decade, you just keep talking, Carl."

His laughter echoed long after they left the room.

"LET'S TAKE A WALK, son," Carl said.

What Linc really wanted to retrieve his cell phone and call Betsey to get his bearings, but perhaps he'd learn something from the old man. "Where are we going?"

"Just a Sunday afternoon stroll. See the sights."

Linc didn't think it kind to point out that you could stand on the front porch of Ivy's café and see most of Palo Verde from there. He'd also never taken a Sunday stroll.

Still, he liked the old guy. So he followed.

"That there, of course, is the courthouse." Carl indicated the tallest building in sight, all of three stories high. "It's number three. First one was built in 1857. Cost three hundred dollars." Carl shook his head. "Can't get a decent TV for that now. 'Course, three hundred dollars was a lot of money back then. Original name of the town was Golconda."

"Why did they change it?"

"Besides it being a mouthful, you mean?" Carl broke out in a big grin. "Well, nobody knows for sure, but my people were here in the beginning, and there's a legend that the county judge got drunk and adjourned court for one hundred years, making it necessary to change the name of the county seat before they could have court again.''

Linc chuckled, ''You believe it?''

Carl shrugged, eyes twinkling. ''Good a story as any, I reckon.'' He pointed to the east. ''About a half-mile down there is my house. First built in 1857 by my great-great-granddaddy. It's called a picket house, and I'm told it's one of the few examples of that type of construction left standing in Texas. Been added onto over the years, but the original walls are still there.''

''What's a picket house?'' The builder in Linc was intrigued.

''Well, see, the way it came down to me, this method originated with the Vikings way back before they invaded what's now Scotland and Ireland. My people are Irish. Come to this country from a sailor shipwrecked off the coast of Virginia in the 1600s. His descendants moved from Virginia to Tennessee, then down to Arkansas and on to Texas.''

His pride bled through his tone. ''When my great-great-granddaddy came before the Civil War, this land was covered with cedar trees. Cedars don't get all that tall, and most don't get very big around, but they were plentiful. The method is sort of like a log cabin, only the posts are placed vertical like a picket fence. Each one is only a few inches thick, and they're mortared together standing up.''

''I'd like to see that. Are any of the original walls visible?''

Carl nodded. ''I kept one section uncovered where the plaster needed work. The original cabin, of course, was only two rooms, and one story high—limited by the height of the posts.''

''They wouldn't take the load of another story, either,'' Linc mused.

Carl nodded, as if to a bright pupil. ''That's right. Any add-ons had to be to the sides.'' He nodded again. ''You want to come by sometime, I'll be glad to show you.''

''Thanks.'' Linc looked around. ''So your roots are here.'' He'd been rootless all his life. He couldn't imagine how that must feel.

''Yep. My people survived Indian raids—some of 'em, anyway. During the Civil War, when most of the menfolk were gone, the women and children would leave home and fort up together until the Indians left the area. It was relatives of mine who were part of the bunch that captured Cynthia Ann Parker, who'd been stolen by Indians and who married Chief Peta Nocona. Her son was the chief Quanah Parker—his eyes were two different colors. Ever heard of him?''

Surprised, Linc nodded. "In Texas history class."

"So you're a Texan?"

Was he? He was born in Texas, but he'd been sent to boarding schools all over and he'd moved often as an adult. Still, he was surprised to realize that, in his heart, Texas really was home. "I was born in Texas," he said carefully.

"Where were you raised?"

"Here and there... So what's this building—?" Linc pointed.

Carl studied him for a minute, then shrugged. "This is the old dry goods store. Ivy's got some idea about turning it into one of them antique malls. Been talking to Lora Lee Johnson about expanding, letting other folks in." Carl walked to the window and peered through the glass. "Only thing antique in there right now is Lora Lee." He slapped his knee and cackled.

Linc grinned and leaned closer. Inside he saw dolls with crocheted dresses, some not very impressive art and a few pieces of furniture caught somewhere between garage-sale era and true antiques, he suspected. "It's closed," he observed. "Wouldn't Sunday be a prime tourist day?"

Carl sighed. "That's what Ivy's been telling folks. Girl's got her hands full, attempting to change their ways."

Linc pretended ignorance. "What's her involvement?"

"She's got some notion to save this town by turning it into a tourist destination, putting on monthly trade days and such. She's got folks coming from Fort Worth and even Dallas as word's getting around about her food. She's trying single-handedly to rescue this town from extinction." His snort made his opinion clear. "Got folks believing she can do it, too, but I suspect the girl's headed for heartbreak. Can't reverse a half century in six months."

"Six months? That's all she's been here?" From the way everyone behaved, he'd assumed she'd lived here for years.

Carl nodded. "She's something, that Ivy girl. Never still a minute…a man's got to wonder what she's running from."

Linc frowned. "Where was she before?"

"Somewhere down by Austin, I think. Got no family but Prudie, I hear tell. I don't know the details and it ain't my business to pry, but something happened down there. Something she don't talk about."

The dead husband. "Would Prudie know?"

"That old bat?" Carl snorted. "She'd just as soon pinch your head off as let you meddle in Ivy's affairs. Girl's all she has in the world. Ivy was lost to her for a lot of years, and Prudie's so glad to have her back she'll take Ivy's story to the grave. Ivy saved her by coming here after Prudie's stroke. Prudie couldn't keep up the café anymore, but it's all she's got left. Ivy's building it back better than it was before. Girl says she won't be here once Prudie's well, but there's a bunch of folks who'll fight to keep her. Maybe she can't get that cheapskate in Dallas to listen, but she's given a lot of folks reason to hope, and that girl won't go down without a fight. She might be small and look harmless, but our Ivy's got grit. She don't give up.''

"What cheapskate in Dallas?'' Though he knew, of course, this was an ideal opportunity to investigate.

"Some lily-livered SOB who's hiding behind a corporation name and a post office box and won't answer Ivy's letters.''

"Maybe there's a good reason.'' Linc wasn't sure why he cared what these people thought. He couldn't let it matter.

Carl snorted anew. "Cheap sonofagun just don't want to face what it would take to make these buildings sound again. It's a family trait.''

Linc bristled but kept quiet.

"Old man Hartwell never cared. It was his wife's people who came from here and loved this place.''

Linc had never heard this version of his family's involvement with this town. Scanning the buildings along this street, knowing that he was responsible for most of them, Linc couldn't disagree that they appeared run-down and badly in need of maintenance but only examining them would tell the tale. "When can we take a look?"

Carl stared at him in surprise. "These folks can't afford to pay you. Ivy can't, either, 'cept for room and board."

Linc chided himself for not remembering his cover better. Carefully, he shrugged. "Just thought maybe I could help Ivy get an idea of what kind of money she's asking to be spent. I've been involved in various aspects of construction since I was eighteen."

"I could use something like that," said a voice from behind them.

Linc turned to see a woman, perhaps in her seventies, hair a startling shade of black.

"This here's Lora Lee Johnson. Meet Linc Garner," Carl said.

The older woman held herself perfectly erect. Dressed to the nines, she even wore the kind of white gloves he hadn't seen on a woman in years. She reminded Linc of a spinster schoolteacher he'd had as a child.

"Pleased to meet you, Mr. Garner. Are you the gentleman who took the fall at Ivy's?"

Linc frowned at his sling. "I am."

"That's a kind thing you tried to do for her. Ivy has her hands full enough without this unwieldy idea of hers."

Linc lifted a brow. "The trade days? Why do you think it won't work?"

The woman glanced through the windows of her store, then back. "Don't get me wrong, Mr. Garner. There are many of us who'd like nothing more than to see Ivy proven right. She's given this town hope that has been sorely lacking. But the heartless fellow who owns all these buildings has not seen fit to give her the courtesy of a response, so I'm less optimistic than our dear Ivy."

"Perhaps there's an explanation for his silence." Linc couldn't help defending himself.

"There's no excuse for such a failure of common decency, young man," Lora Lee sniffed. "The least he could do is respond, even if it's to say no."

Garner's death was the obvious excuse, but Linc could see that Garner had ignored this place for years. The builder in Linc loathed the decay and neglect he saw here. He wondered what his great-grandfather Hartwell would say about the fate of the town that had given him his start.

Linc opened his mouth to explain, but the memory of Betsey's green eyes, glistening with tears, stopped him. Betsey was as much an innocent in this as Ivy. She'd had enough hard knocks. He didn't need to be saying anything about the landlord until he had a solution.

It didn't take an expert to see that the wood was so long without paint, the elements had eaten away at the fine molding. To see that the windowpanes had pulled away from their frames. To imagine the dry rot claiming the foundations of buildings standing upright only because their neighbors provided support.

How long before the entire town fell apart, a victim of time and weather and neglect?

And how could one small woman think she could reverse any of that?

A new image shimmered before him—Ivy, small and fierce, a catch in her breath as she held him still in the chair with the determination of someone twice her size. She was kidding herself that she could reverse what fate had dealt this town, but he did not relish being the one to tell her so.

It had to be done in stages, he decided. He would offer to assess what needed to be done to bring the town's buildings up to modern standards. As the evidence mounted, surely even a cockeyed optimist like Ivy would see that the task was unrealistic.

But even as he thought it, he realized that he liked Ivy's optimism, liked in her what Carl called "grit." All the more reason to have an alternative ready for her—a new location in which he could leave her safely, knowing she would be sure to succeed when he'd gone back to the life he'd made....

"If you have a moment, Mrs. Johnson, I'd be glad to look around and assess the repairs that should be done."

"Why, thank you, young man." Her lips parted in a smile. "Mabel told me you were a gentleman, and I see that she was right." Then she winked at him. "Our Ivy could do worse than a beau like you."

Before a shocked Linc could set her straight, she turned away, drawing a key from her purse.

Carl chuckled and nudged Linc with an elbow to the ribs.

Then he and Lora Lee Johnson walked inside, leaving a speechless Linc to follow.

CHAPTER FIVE

"MAGGIE." Linc spoke into his cell phone, long past caring that he'd interrupted her Sunday. He was parked under a shade tree, a mile south of town on Highway 4, having made his escape by saying he needed to buy gas for his truck.

"Hey, boss man, what's shakin'?" Maggie might be in her fifties, but she dressed like a teenager and spoke in an odd mix of new and old slang. "You don't sound so good. Life in the sticks getting to you?"

"You have no idea." Linc leaned back against the seat. "Look, I'm sorry to bother you on the weekend, but—"

Maggie halted him in mid-sentence with a raucous laugh. "I expected this call hours ago. I'm surprised you made it through the night, boss, if you want the honest truth."

Linc frowned. "I try to leave you alone on weekends since you and Bart—"

"Shacked up?" Maggie suggested. Then she laughed again.

Men came to complete and total attention when that laugh erupted. Linc had seen the population of an entire lumberyard converge on Maggie's location just because of that laugh. In fact, it was where he had found her, working cashier in an effort to keep body and soul and an ailing father together.

He paid Maggie well—very well—now. She could retire today and be set for life. But her worth to him was far beyond the job she did. She'd never stopped trying to make him slow down, never stopped reminding him, when he got too intense, that work was only a means, not an end.

He didn't always agree, but that didn't mean he didn't appreciate her. Rough and rowdy as she was, Maggie had been the kindest person in Linc Galloway's life for the past fifteen years.

"So what can I do you for, big boss man?"

Linc's mouth quirked at her irreverence. He let out a long breath and closed his eyes for a second. "The situation here is…complicated. Ivy Parker's not what I expected."

"More of a dingbat or less?"

Linc bristled in Ivy's defense. "She's not a dingbat."

There was a slight pause. "O-o-kay," Maggie said. "So tell me about her."

"Don't use that indulgent tone on me, Maggie—'' He sat up too quickly and bumped his shoulder. "Ow—damn it—"

"What is it?"

"Nothing—just dislocated my shoulder falling off Ivy's ladder."

"Dislocated?" A long pause followed. "I told you those fancy suits would be the death of you." There was a grin in her voice.

He'd been a fledgling builder when they'd met, but he'd already known that his future lay with his mind, not his hands.

"Too much easy livin', boss."

Linc grinned, too. "I still know how to climb a ladder. I was just distracted."

"How old is this Ivy Parker?" Maggie's tone sharpened. When he didn't answer, she went on. "She's young, isn't she."

"Maybe thirty."

"Good-looking, right?"

Linc sighed. "Beautiful. Long blond hair and these amazing blue eyes that—"

"Sounds like she's getting to you," Maggie interrupted.

He sat up straight. "Of course she's not. It's just that she's so damn innocent and…sweet."

"Sweet," Maggie said carefully. "Innocent…. Not exactly your type."

"There's nothing like that happening."

"What's your father going to think?"

Maggie had disliked his family on principle ever since the long-ago evening when she and he had celebrated a milestone with too many drinks and Linc had told her about his lost love and broken family ties, a story he'd never shared with anyone. Maggie didn't think he owed his family anything.

But now Garner was dead.

And Betsey needed him.

"There's nothing for him to think," he said coldly. "I'm going to take care of Betsey. I owe Garner that and more."

"You're not responsible, boss."

Linc closed his eyes. "Then who the hell is?"

"Your father threw you out, remember? Didn't even bother to tell you when your brother died, until he was desperate for your help."

"It doesn't matter, Maggie. I'm not doing this for him. I'm doing it for my brother. I knew where he was. I should have checked, should have been aware that he was in trouble. Garner set impossible standards for himself, trying to please my father."

"You set some pretty impossible ones for yourself." Maggie sighed. "Betsey called, by the way. Wants to talk to you. Says it's urgent."

"Why didn't you phone me right away?"

"Podunk Paradise doesn't get good reception. I couldn't even get your voice mail."

Linc frowned. "Is the reception okay now?"

"Crystal."

"I can't afford to leave the phone on. Ivy thinks I'm dead broke."

"You'll be back today anyway, right?"

"Well…"

"Spill it, boss. What's going on?"

Linc didn't know how to explain about Ivy or her dreams, about Carl and his family history, about Lora Lee's faint hopes. "I can't leave yet. I need more information. I have to stay another day or so."

"Lots of stuff's coming to a boil, Linc. We need you here."

Knowing she was right didn't help. "Keeping things running is why I pay you well."

"Yes, sir." Hurt reverberated in her tone.

Linc cursed beneath his breath. "I'm sorry, Maggie. This is a hell of a mess, and I'm trying to figure my way out of it so everyone can win."

"Including Ivy Parker?"

His jaw clenched. What had he been thinking? He should just leave now, sell the buildings and get on with his life. It was the only logical choice.

But the memory of a flour-dusted curve of cheek stopped him. "I need you to get me a list of locations for a restaurant in Dallas."

"Serving what kind of food?"

"The best you ever ate," he responded. "Biscuits that could make Satan convert, pie that would have you believing in Santa Claus again—"

"So it's the food that's keeping you there?"

Linc remembered the press of soft breasts. Remembered kind blue eyes and a woman with a need to save lost lambs.

"Yeah," he answered. "It's the food. Dallasites will go nuts over it. We'll find a better location for her, and she won't care what happens to the buildings in this hick town."

"So that'll solve your problem?" Maggie asked.

Linc stared out the windshield of the pickup, back toward Palo Verde, and reminded himself of all the reasons he needed to be gone from here right away. "Yeah," he said, pinching the bridge of his nose. "That'll take care of it."

"Good," she said. "The engineer decided to redraw the plans for that new subdivision, and the Meadows deal's looking hinky. We need you back ASAP."

He knew it was true. Staying here made no sense. "Give me a couple of days, Maggie. And get me that list first thing in the morning." Yeah, that was it. He'd find a property for Ivy and they'd be square. He felt better already. "Now tell me what's going on with the Sampson deal."

For several minutes they tossed around details

and strategies, and Linc felt like himself again. His blood hummed with competitive juices. It was great thinking about business and not messy emotions, even if some of the information Maggie provided made him all too aware that he needed to get back, full-time, to his real life—or face severe consequences.

"Thanks, Mag," he said. "You're irreplaceable, you know."

Maggie snorted. "Yeah, I know, boss man. Just want to be sure you don't forget. I'll remind you next month when it's time to cut payroll checks."

Linc laughed and started to hang up. He paused for just a minute. "And tell Betsey I'll call her tomorrow. My battery's running low."

Even as the lie passed his lips, Linc wondered what was wrong with him.

IVY PULLED THE SHEETS from the clothesline with a snap, then folded them with brisk efficiency and carried them, still warm from the sunshine, up the stairs of what she hoped would become a thriving bed-and-breakfast. With quick strides, she crossed the creaky wood floors to the only guest room close to being finished. She'd polished the floors to a glow and moved in an antique walnut bed and chest. Beside the bed she'd placed an oval rag rug she'd bought from Lora Lee. Stepping onto it now as she spread the sheet over the mattress, she wondered about the woman who'd made the rug. Where had she lived? Had she made it for a beloved child or for the warmth of a hearth? Had the home it graced been filled with love and laughter?

Ivy tucked the sheets into hospital corners and slipped a faded log cabin quilt atop it all, then fluffed the pillows at the head of the bed.

"My mother pieced that quilt," said Aunt Prudie from the doorway. "It's been here all along, all those years I've been gone."

Aunt Prudie had married a navy man, and until his death ten years ago, she'd traveled the world with him. They'd never had children, so she'd never needed to stay in one place.

"You missed it, didn't you," Ivy said.

Prudie nodded. "Never expected to, not when I was young and so in love. Broke my mother's heart, I did, never realizing how much she might pine for her only daughter."

"But she saved it for you."

Prudie shrugged. "And then I lost it." Her husband's lingering terminal illness had eaten up all their savings and required the sale of her mother's family home, just when Prudie had finally realized that, through all her travels, she'd always thought she'd wind up home again.

"It couldn't be helped, Auntie," Ivy soothed. "She would have understood."

"I don't think so." Her aunt shook her head. "Mama barely got as far as Mineral Wells. She couldn't see why I couldn't find what I wanted here." Her eyes glistened. "And if I'd stayed, the home place would still be in the family. I'd have something to pass down to you, child, besides troubles."

Ivy couldn't stand the sorrow in the older woman's voice. She crossed the floor. "You've given me much more than that. You've given me a family again."

Prudie shook her head. "I should have kept in touch. If I'd been here, I could have taken you girls in. Kept you together. I never even met little Chloe. She was born when we were in Japan."

Ivy thought of her baby sister, only four when they were separated. Chloe's adoption records had been sealed and her trail gone cold. Their sister Caroline, sixteen to her thirteen back then, had run away from foster care after only four months, Ivy had discovered. She'd vanished like mist. It would take more time and a lot of money to find either one, but Ivy refused to be deterred. She'd lost all the family she intended to lose. "I'm going to find them both, Aunt Prudie. Never you worry about that."

"Sell this business, honey. Use the money to search for your sisters."

Ivy wished that were an option, but her aunt had never had a home base. They were only tenants here, and Ivy's hopes had expanded to include finding a way to buy this place and ensure that Aunt Prudie would never have to move again. "I can't, Auntie. People are depending on me." She smiled past her ache. "Besides, if we closed down, when would Carl have a chance to flirt with you?"

Her tiny aunt's cheeks went bright with color. "Oh, get on with you. That old man is more trouble than he's worth. And I'm long past flirting." But as always, her vehemence lacked a certain edge.

"I think Carl would make a splendid beau," Ivy declared.

Her aunt's pin curls bounced as she shook her head. "He's twice as ornery as my uncle's billy goat and half as smart. Anyway—" she sniffed "—I'm an old woman now. It's past my time."

Before Ivy could protest, her aunt went on. "Now, if we're going to talk about beaux, that Linc Garner would make a fine one. Mabel and I've been watching you two and we agree that you'd make beautiful babies between you."

Ivy recoiled as if she'd been slapped. All humor fled. "It's only been ten months, Auntie," she whispered. "I can't think about babies yet—if ever." She busied herself plumping pillows that didn't need it.

"Oh, child, I'm sorry. I know you're hurting, but you've got to let go and get on with life."

"I am getting on," Ivy said tightly. "I stay busy."

"Yes, you do," the older woman said. "But you haven't let go." Her voice lowered. "You've got to cry, child. You've got to say goodbye. I've lost four babies, and I know how you're feeling."

Ivy turned, astounded. "You? I—I didn't realize."

"I wanted children more than anything, but the good Lord didn't see fit to bless us with them. Each time I lost one was like tearing off a piece of my heart and burying it in cold ground." She raised tear-bright eyes to Ivy. "You never forget the lost ones, Ivy, but you don't let it stop you from living. You won't be like me—there can't be justice in the world if a natural-born mother like you can't have children. The shock and grief of what that no-good did was to blame. You'll have other children, if you'll just give yourself a chance. I truly believe that."

"I wish I could," Ivy murmured from her deepest longings. "But I'm so afraid, Auntie. The doctor couldn't say why it happened, why the bleeding started. He said the next time would likely be fine, but he couldn't promise it wouldn't happen again." Her voice dropped to a whisper. "I wanted that baby so much." She began smoothing the sheets again. "I can't say goodbye yet. I can't just walk away."

She straightened, glancing out the window at her garden. "I want to gather some rosemary. I think it will give the room a nice scent without being fussy or flowery. What do you think?" She stared at her aunt, daring her to re-open the subject that was Ivy's deepest wound.

Her aunt's eyes were soft and sad, but she let the subject drop. "Some sage might be nice, too."

Ivy smiled her gratitude. "Can I help you back to your room?"

Aunt Prudie shook her head. "No, sweetheart. I'll be fine. You go on."

But just as Ivy passed her in the doorway, she felt a faint touch on her arm and glanced at her aunt.

"My story won't be your story, Ivy. You give life a chance, you hear? You'll find that right man and have those babies if you just don't close off your heart. And we'll find your sisters, too, you'll see."

Ivy shook her head, unable to speak past the lump in her throat. With hasty steps, she descended the stairs.

IT WAS ALMOST NIGHT when Linc returned. The café windows were dark, and he almost got in his truck again to return to the life he knew. He could be in Dallas in a couple of hours, back in his hotel room. Or he could rouse his pilot, have his plane winging toward Denver and be home before midnight. Be in his own bed once more before morning.

Regardless of the tangled mess Linc was needed to unravel, his father didn't really want him around. Never had, despite a young boy's longings.

Linc spared a smile for that boy and his brother, whose rearing had been left up to a succession of housekeepers and boarding schools, where Linc had usually succeeded in getting himself thrown out.

Garner had taken the opposite tack, getting good grades, endearing himself to teachers—which had only made Linc look worse. Over the years their relationship had hardened into a duel for their father's scant attention. Linc had won a brief, stunning victory when he'd run off with Garner's intended wife. When Betsey lost her nerve, he'd taken her home and watched her accept the life for which she'd been bred. His father had noticed him then, all right, his fury a laser slicing Linc out of their lives like a cancer.

His father needed his skills now, but he was only tolerated, his past misdeeds unforgiven.

But as he rounded the building, flirting with the thought of returning to the life he'd fashioned to suit himself, Linc caught a glimpse of pale fabric glowing against the shadows. A small figure bending over the nearly black plant shapes.

Ivy. In her garden.

Linc stopped and watched her for a minute, slipping between rows like some wraith. Only, he knew better. Ivy was no wraith; she was the most alive of any person he'd ever met.

She flitted from plant to plant, bending to pinch here, stooping to snip away there. Over one arm, she carried a basket rapidly filling with greenery.

Only Ivy would be gardening by moonglow. Carl was right—the woman never rested.

Did she, too, have her demons?

"Ivy."

"Oh—" she gasped, straightening to face him. "I—I didn't know anyone was—"

"Sit down," Linc ordered.

"I beg your pardon?" Frost quickly replaced surprise.

"Take a minute. Put your feet up. Do you ever just sit and relax?"

"I relax," she said, glancing away and moving to pinch another leaf.

Linc laughed. "I never thought I'd find anyone who worked more than I did. Maggie—" He halted, startled at what he'd almost given away.

"Is Maggie your wife or girlfriend?"

He didn't answer.

Ivy looked away. "Never mind. It's none of my business."

"I'm not married." He wasn't sure why he wanted her to know that.

"It doesn't matter." Ivy shrugged. "Let me show you to your room."

"Room?"

"In the bed-and-breakfast—well, what will become the bed-and-breakfast. You'll be my first guest."

"You don't have to go to all this trouble."

"You're paying your way, never fear." Ivy's eyes twinkled. "I'm making up my list. You may decide the price is too high."

Linc resolved to give her more than her money's worth, in apology for what he would have to do to her. His talk with Maggie had reminded him as nothing else could that he wasn't here for anything but business. As soon as he could gracefully make his escape, he'd be gone. Ivy Parker and Linc Galloway lived in two separate worlds.

"Second thoughts?" she teased.

"What? Oh—no. Woolgathering." He nodded toward the main building. "Is my room up there?"

Ivy nodded. "Come on. I'll show you."

He glanced at her full basket. "I don't want to interrupt."

"I'm through. Just gathering some rosemary for your room and some basil to dry for use this winter. I'll gather more in the morning to make pesto for lunch. Sound good?"

"I'm hungry already." Which was more than the truth, since he hadn't eaten since noon.

"You missed supper. Come on," she said, picking up her pace. "I'll put together a plate for you."

"I wasn't hinting, and you've already worked enough for one day. Just point me toward what's allowable, and I'll make myself a sandwich or something."

"That, Mr. Garner, is not part of our deal. I said room and board, and I meant it."

"Even if the boarder doesn't show up in time to eat?"

"Even if," she said firmly. "Follow me."

And so it was that Linc found himself heading back down toward the kitchen after stopping by his room to shower away the day and to test out the bed, which was a little short for his height but would suit well enough. The scent he noted must have been the rosemary, but beneath it he caught a whiff of something that smelled like sunshine, and he realized it came from the sheets.

He'd never slept on sheets dried in the sunshine. Never dreamed anyone still did something he'd only read about in books.

Stomach rumbling in anticipation of more of Ivy's food, Linc headed down the stairs.

IVY FELT HIM before she heard his footsteps. Chiding herself mentally for the shiver that ran through her, she composed herself and faced him.

But as always, she wasn't prepared for the impact of his sheer physical presence.

Long muscular legs gloved in another worn pair of jeans, his broad chest filling a plain white T-shirt as though tailor-made for him, Linc walked into the room with an air of quiet command. He'd removed the bandages, keeping only the sling. She knew better than to lecture.

He paused a few feet away, his gray eyes warm but troubled, and she longed, for one foolish moment, for things she could not have.

Turning too quickly, she grazed the hot pan with her thumb, and hissed with pain.

"Here." His deep voice rumbled. "Let me see." With fingers both strong and gentle, he held her hand, and Ivy couldn't help a quick intake of breath at the touch of his flesh.

He misunderstood. "I'm sorry. I didn't mean to hurt you—"

"You didn't," she murmured. "You—" Jerking her hand away, Ivy fumbled with the refrigerator, seeking a cube of ice.

"Let me help you," he said, reaching past her. Clasping two cubes of ice in one hand, he picked up her hand with the other. Slowly and carefully, he began to stroke over the burn.

Ivy bit her bottom lip against the contrast—his warm flesh, the icy sting…and again, the awareness flowing like a current between them.

Staring at his bent head, the fingers of her other hand itching to see if his hair was as soft as she remembered, Ivy studied the lines of his proud head, the breadth of his strong shoulders.

When she wanted to curl her body against his, instead she straightened the fabric strip that tied his sling. "Should you be using that hand?" she asked, desperate for distraction.

He looked up from the burn, and the movement brought his face only inches from hers.

His gaze dropped to her lips, and Ivy closed her eyes against temptation.

He narrowed the gap. With one slow brush, Linc's lips met hers.

Ivy gasped, and his tongue traced the tender inner edge of her lips. For a second, treacherous and precious, she wanted to yield, to invite him inside—

Instead, she whirled away, jarring his injured arm. Hearing his muffled groan, she recoiled. "I'm sorry. I shouldn't—you—we—" Embarrassed at how she'd let down her guard, Ivy grappled with the plate she'd prepared and bumped against the hot pan again.

The plate dropped from her fingers, but Linc caught it just in time. "Hey," he soothed. "I'm sorry. I had no right."

"No." She turned to the table, almost knocking the fork to the floor. "It's my—I shouldn't—" Finally, she gave up. "Just eat, all right? Put your plate in the sink, and I'll clean up in the morning. Good night."

And with that, she fled to the safety of her little cottage and her empty bed.

CHAPTER SIX

LINC CLIMBED DOWN from Lora Lee's attic and rotated his shoulder. He'd gone without the sling this morning and so far, so good. Tender, yes, but nothing he couldn't handle. Heavy lifting would have to wait, but he'd been relieved to find himself good to go.

"Well, young man?" Lora Lee peered up at him from behind her desk. "Are you sure you shouldn't still have that shoulder wrapped?"

Linc bit back a terse response. So far today, Mabel, Aunt Prudie and Carl had all asked the same thing. Only Ivy had been mute on the subject, but then, Ivy had made herself scarce this morning, sending his breakfast via Mabel and nowhere in evidence when he sought her out. The café had been busy, but no more so than he'd seen it before. Commuters to jobs in Weatherford and Fort Worth came early, followed by the courthouse crowd, and farmers and ranchers who would have already completed early chores, Carl said. The diner was a small place, but it did a decent business between locals and travelers passing through. He'd heard a retired couple from Fort Worth tell Mabel they'd driven over solely for Ivy's breakfast biscuits.

Ivy should have been out there to hear it, instead of hiding in the kitchen. He could only assume she was avoiding him after last night's close call, and frankly, that was just fine with him. He'd been a damn fool to yield to the temptation she'd presented, and he'd had a restless night because of it. Too much sleep had fled as he remembered the feel of her lips and wondered how it would be to turn a chaste kiss into something more.

But considering the punch of what he'd once have called barely a kiss, Linc wasn't eager to take things further.

Oh, hell. That was a lie. He wanted to take things all the way, wanted Ivy beneath him, uttering more of those catchy little breaths and soul-deep sighs as he—

"Young man?" Lora Lee prodded.

He jolted. *Get your mind on what's important, Linc.* "Ms. Johnson, I have mixed news for you. Which would you like first?"

"I've always believed in confronting life squarely. Get one's work done first and then recreate. I always told my students the same thing."

Bingo. Linc suppressed a grin. "You were a schoolteacher?"

"Forty-five years. I taught mathematics."

Linc nodded. "I'll bet you were a good one."

Her eyes warmed. "I like to believe so. Sometimes students will write me or visit to tell me that they still remember me. It's my consolation for never having married or had children."

"Are you sorry you never married or had children?"

A small shadow crossed her face. "I would have liked to do so, yes. I was once engaged, but he died in the Korean War."

"Never found anyone to replace him?"

She stiffened. "I never tried. I believe there is one true love for each of us and no more."

"The math teacher is a romantic?" He softened any sting with a grin.

The older woman smiled back. "It isn't a popular view in these cynical times, I know, but true love exists. There are values that are timeless, and we are poorer as a people if we try to deny them. The stories that have sustained mankind for generations do so for a reason—because values such as love and honor and truth are real, and they are crucial to man's survival. In this modern age, too much is focused on money and power and possessions. None of them satisfy cravings in us that are soul-deep—" She broke off, her cheeks pink. "I'm sorry. Apparently the pedant in me does not retire easily.''

But Linc was struck by the glow that passionate belief had lit in her eyes. For a moment, he thought he could see the young woman who'd been so in love that she'd carried one man in her heart for all her long life. ''You really believe that we only have one true love?'' He pondered the young Betsey and how she'd consumed all his thoughts.

''I do.'' Lora Lee nodded. ''Oh, there can be infatuations. But the heart longs for that one deep bond. No matter how difficult the road to stake claim on that love, if one turns away, the heart will always be incomplete.''

Was that the source of the shadows he'd seen in Ivy's eyes? Had she lost her one true love?

Linc shook his head. ''No disrespect meant, Ms. Johnson, but I think your case was the exception, not the rule. Some of us do fine without that.''

She smiled at him sadly. '' 'Fine' is cold comfort on long, dark nights, Mr. Garner.'' She peered at him. ''I suspect you know what I mean.''

Linc drew back from that too-close arrow. ''I like my life just the way it is.''

''I wonder,'' she murmured, then shook her head. ''But that is neither here nor there. Tell me what you've found.''

Relieved to move back into the world of the physical, Linc began to list all that was wrong with her building. To bring it to anything that remotely resembled compliance with modern building codes would take thousands of dollars. This should start to convince Ivy to abandon her game plan.

"Seems to me," he said, "that the landlord would surely have to raise rents drastically to cover that sort of expenditure."

Lora Lee's face had paled during his recitation. "Yes, I can see that."

Linc felt like a heel as he watched her. She was old and had suffered a great loss in her life. She was alone, trying to make ends meet when she probably subsisted on scant retirement funds. "I could—"

Her head lifted; her eyes filled with hope. "You could what?"

Linc looked away. What could he do? He didn't own these buildings. His father and Betsey didn't have the money to fix them up. He tried hard to pull Betsey's tear-filled eyes into focus. *Betsey*. He was here to pay a debt to his brother, not for any of these people.

Linc forced himself to face her, feeling lower than low. "I could write you up a list if you want."

"Perhaps later." She sounded weary. "Right

now, I must see to my shop.'' Rising from her chair, she grasped a feather duster, moving toward a set of bric-a-brac shelves.

"Ms. Johnson, I—"

She turned a brave smile on him, her eyes old and sad and wise. "It's not your fault, young man. You didn't create this situation. And poor Ivy didn't mean to generate false hopes. Life is seldom fair. I'll admit that I was beginning to warm to her idea, but—'' She shrugged, then straightened shoulders that had rounded under the weight of age and life's disappointments. "Thank you for your time, Mr. Garner. What do I owe you?"

Linc could have crawled beneath the belly of a snake and still had clearance. "Not a thing, ma'am. I just wish—'' What? Hell, he'd wished for things to be different all his life and it hadn't had any effect. "I wish I had better news."

"You told me the truth, and that's all I wanted. I thank you for that."

Linc said goodbye and left, correcting his earlier thought. He'd require a stepladder to reach up to a snake's belly right now.

And this building was just the beginning.

Betsey. Remember Garner's widow.

With long strides, Linc headed for his truck. He needed to make a call to remind himself that what

he was doing would be good for someone. Someone he'd promised help to long before he'd ever
heard the name Ivy Parker.

IVY SAT ON THE FLOOR of the café, playing patty-
cake with Stevie.

"Okay, hon, see you tomorrow," Mabel called.
"Register's all counted out, and I'll drop these de-
posits off at the bank on my way home."

"Thank you, Mabel. I appreciate you making
the trip."

"No trouble, hon. Just—"

"Just what?"

Mabel paused. "You sure you're all right?
You've been awful quiet today."

"I'm fine," Ivy pasted on a smile.

Mabel stared at her for a moment. "Send that
child home and take yourself a nap. I could pack
a week's worth of clothes in those bags under your
eyes."

Ivy resisted the urge to head for a mirror.
"Thanks a lot."

"Oh, you look beautiful as always, hon, just...
tired. Bone tired. Dog tired."

Sometimes Ivy wasn't sure she remembered what
rested felt like. Last night's tossing and turning
hadn't helped. She'd finally gotten up and read until

almost dawn, trying to replace the too-vivid memory of Linc Garner's kiss with something. Anything.

"I'm fine, Mabel, really. Just a little short on sleep last night, but I'll catch up tonight."

"Humph," the older woman muttered. "Prudie never asked you to kill yourself for her. She's ready to pitch in again, and you'd best let her."

Ivy stifled a small beat of panic at the thought that one day soon, her aunt wouldn't need her help. Then what would she do? Where would she go?

"We'll be fine, Mabel," she reiterated. "Thank you for taking the deposit." She turned back to the chubby toddler sitting before her.

"Baby's rubbing her eyes," Mabel noted. "Seems like one of you knows when a nap's needed."

"Yes, *Mother*." Ivy grimaced.

Mabel grinned. "That's the spirit. Have a good nap, little girl." She waved and walked out the door.

Ivy looked down at the toddler. "Ready to rock a little, Stevie girl? How about a lullaby?" Gathering the child in her arms, Ivy rose to her feet and began to sing.

"LINC! How are you? Why aren't you back?" Betsey said.

The delight in her tone warmed him. Linc settled

into the seat to enjoy the contact with his real life. "How are you, Bets? You sound good." He hadn't heard this much vigor in her tone since he'd returned to Dallas.

"I miss you," she said in a way he would have sold his soul to hear fifteen years ago. "When are you coming home?"

Home. Dallas wasn't his home; Denver was. But hearing the words was welcome. For the first time in three days, Linc felt he had his feet under him again.

"Soon."

"How soon? Why can't you come back now? I need you, Linc."

She needed him. She wanted him home. Linc looked around him at the scenic view of the Palo Verde Mountains and wished suddenly that the miles between Dallas and here would simply vanish.

In two hours, he could be there. He could call Ivy when he got back and—

And what? Tell her he'd lied to her? Tell her he'd lied to all of them? That he had no solutions, that she simply had to give up her dream? *Tough luck, kid—so long—see you around?*

Thick dark lashes drifting shut over sweet blue eyes...full pink lips barely parted—

"Linc?"

Linc shot up straight in the seat. He had no business remembering one kiss so light it wouldn't even have registered that high on the Richter scale. Betsey had to be his only concern.

"How's my father?" he asked, scrambling to send Ivy back where she belonged.

"He needs you, too, Linc."

Linc snorted. "He's never needed me. He needs my business acumen to get him out of the hole his perfect son dug—" At Betsey's soft gasp, he blew out a breath. "God, I'm sorry. I didn't mean—" He fell silent.

After a minute she spoke. "How bad is it?"

He'd like to be able to talk honestly with her and reason out a solution, but Betsey wasn't like Ivy. Where Ivy would take a blow and keep moving, Betsey shattered.

"I can't tell yet. I have to look around a little more."

"But what about the opera benefit?"

"What about it?"

"I—You said you'd go with me."

Linc sighed. The circles of Dallas society held no appeal for him. Garner had loved it. "Bets, I—"

"That's all right. Don't worry about it."

Suddenly, Linc remembered that Betsey was the

chairman of that benefit. She'd worked hard on it for months, his father's secretary had said.

"When is it again?"

"Saturday night."

Saturday. Five days from now. He could wrap this up by then. "I'll be there. Call Maggie for me and make sure she has my tux sent down, will you?"

"Are you sure, Linc? You don't have to—"

"I'm sure. Garner would want you to go."

She didn't answer right away. When she did, her voice was low and haunted. "Linc, I keep thinking that if I'd paid more attention—"

"Don't, Bets." He cut her off. "It doesn't help."

"But—"

He couldn't discuss it yet, not now. Not with her. "Call Maggie and give her the address and what time to pick you up."

"Linc, it wasn't your fault, either. You had no way to know."

And I kept it that way.

"I'll see you, Bets."

"Linc…"

"What?" Even he could hear the abruptness.

"I'm glad you're coming home soon," she said. "And not just for me. Your father is weaker.

He really wants to talk to you, but he won't tell me why."

One more reason to leave Palo Verde sooner rather than later. "Tell him I'll be back by Friday at the latest, sooner if I can. He's not that weak, right?"

"No. He's not doing well but he's holding steady."

"Call me if that changes."

"I will."

"'Bye, Bets."

"Hurry home, Linc. I know I should be able to manage all this by myself, but…"

"You're doing fine," he murmured.

"Linc, wait—" Her tone was breathy…intimate.

For a second, he imagined she would finish their conversation with words he'd waited years to hear. Words he'd have thought he'd welcome.

"I'm sorry for being so much trouble. And for…everything."

It was the closest they'd come to a discussion of their past. In the years since he'd been gone, he'd had plenty of time to think about Betsey's betrayal. He saw now how young she'd been and what a poor prospect he'd presented. For a girl who'd spent her entire life toeing the line, running away with the bad seed had required extraordinary courage. Exile would have destroyed her, but he'd been too angry and young to see that. She'd been born and bred to conform, to carve out a nice, neat, acceptable life. She'd always been pampered and taken care of; she'd never be like—

Ivy. The comparison made him smile. Betsey Wilson Galloway would never have flour on her cheek, never take in a stranger.

But he owed her. He still had feelings for her. First love might be foolish and impulsive, but it left footprints on your heart.

"You haven't done anything wrong, Betsey."

"Oh, Linc…"

"I'll see you soon," he said gently. Before she could respond, he closed the phone.

Nearing town a few minutes later, he tried to figure out what he'd say to Ivy. Nothing came. The deal maker had run out of words. For a moment, he considered just driving on, but he couldn't do that to Ivy.

He wanted to see her. He wasn't ready to say goodbye yet.

At the café, Linc looked in the kitchen first, but it was empty. Then he heard the sound of singing coming from the dining room and crossed the floor toward it.

In the doorway he stopped cold at the sight that greeted him. In the middle of the deserted dining room, Ivy danced, a sleeping baby in her arms. Her movements were a grace note, her voice soft and sweet. Her back was to him, and he watched the sway of her hips until the words began to sink in.

He'd heard this song before...

Tendrils of memory stirred. Linc could recall only a darkened room and the satin of wood against his arm, the press of warmth...the slow rocking and sense of safety, of being cherished—

His mother. She had sung this song to him, a fretful small boy who often had trouble falling to sleep. Linc had few memories of his mother, who had died when he was barely six, and he'd never had this one before. But he knew as well as he knew his own name that the memory was real.

Once he had been loved. He'd known what this small girl knew now, the feeling of safety. Of real peace.

The feeling of home.

Raw from his discussion with Betsey, he took one step toward the oasis. The floorboard creaked.

Ivy turned, and he saw tears hovering on her lashes.

He stepped back from a moment too private to intervene. Ivy looked right at him, and for countless seconds, time ceased.

Linc couldn't speak; there were no words for how this felt. Intimate, surely. Almost sacred. He was a trespasser who had no right to cross over into Ivy's world—

No matter how she called to him, no matter how something inside him yearned—

Ivy's lips parted slightly. In her eyes, he saw messages older than time. Hope and comfort and longing...

For one endless moment, Linc battled temptation. She was like nothing he'd ever seen before, like no one he'd ever met. Before a foolish, long-dead boy could make a grown man yield to impulses that would only make this kind woman suffer more, Linc remembered who he was and what he owed.

And made himself walk out the door.

CHAPTER SEVEN

IVY SAT in the creaky porch swing, stationery and pen idle on her lap desk, one leg swinging absently as she tried to think of a new way to get the landlord's attention.

But her concentration, usually so effortless, came hard today. Every time she thought about the buildings, she thought of the man whose bedroom window she could see from here. For two days now, Linc had made himself scarce, working from sunup to sundown, going over the other buildings on the square. Lora Lee praised his work on the temperamental back-door lock he'd repaired with only the tools in his pickup. Carl applauded his thoroughness in testing electrical circuits and inspecting plumbing, expressing concern that Linc had exerted himself too much climbing up on roofs and into dark crawl spaces.

Ivy worried, too. She could see how he favored his shoulder when he thought no one was looking, so she hadn't yet given him her own wish list of repairs.

He was a stubborn man, she was coming to re-alize. Quiet. Self-contained. Intense. He moved about upstairs in the B and B so noiselessly that she could easily forget he was there. He arrived at the café, ate his meals without lingering, then headed back out on the square. He hadn't spoken a word to her since—

Ivy's fingers tightened on the pen. He'd become more elusive than ever since he'd come in while she was singing Stevie to sleep. She'd been lost in the song, in the pure pleasure of a child's welcome weight against her breast, all powder scented and rosy cheeked and trusting. She'd opened her eyes to find Linc watching her with a look on his face that would break the hardest of hearts.

Pain, she'd seen there, raw and deep. Pain…and a bittersweet longing.

For what did he long, this complicated man? Who had hurt him? Of what did he dream?

She would likely never know. He was only a drifter passing through. She couldn't afford to get attached.

But in that moment before he'd slammed the doors shut on his heart and turned away, the power of that naked yearning had shocked her.

She wanted to understand that pain. Wanted to soothe it away.

But he was a grown man and a proud one, and

he hadn't asked for her help. Wouldn't like knowing that she'd seen.

Sighing, she looked back down at the sheet of flowered stationery on which she'd only inscribed the date and To Whom It May Concern.

She threw the pen down in disgust. What kind of name was that? Why couldn't she at least find out a name? Was that so much to ask? A simple name. Dear Mr. Jones. Dear Mr. Smith. Something, anything—

"Well, he can't just—" Leaping to her feet in pique, Ivy whirled toward the porch steps—

And ran right into Linc's very broad chest.

"Whoa," Linc said, grasping her upper arms to steady her. When she lifted her head, he was both surprised and amused by the temper sparking in those blue eyes. "Who can't just what?"

"I'm sick of it, do you hear me? What kind of coward is he, hiding behind some post office box? What kind of man just lets his property fall into ruin and takes a whole town with it? What kind of—"

"Who are you talking about? The landlord? How do you know it's a man?" Linc asked.

That brought her up short. Blue eyes went wide. "I— Well, I guess I don't." She tossed her everpresent ponytail, then stepped away from him to pace the length of the creaking porch timbers. "Anyway, it doesn't matter. What matters is—''

"You should put that on your list," he noted.

"He—or she—should have the common decency—'' She spun to face him. "What? Put what on my list?''

Linc nodded toward the wide planks. "This porch doesn't seem any too sound. I'll take a look at it, and then you're going to give me your list. You're feeding me and housing me, and you still haven't given me your list. I told you I don't take charity.'' He didn't like owing anyone, and continuing this deception weighed on him.

She stopped pacing and crossed her arms over her stomach. "Your shoulder should still be immobilized. You have no business doing all that climbing around buildings.''

His overall level of frustration was already high enough without his having to endure being lectured. He could hear Maggie's voice in his head after their most recent conversation, not understanding why he was neglecting his own business, why he was still hanging around when the verdict was clear. On top of that, Betsey had called twice more, asking plaintively if he couldn't return sooner. He could solve everything if the Sampson deal would come through or if Ivy would just give up on a lost cause—and instead, here she was, scolding him as though she were his mother.

He was a man accustomed to power and control, and he'd lost both. Somehow this little bit of woman he barely knew had made him feel things he didn't want to feel, damn it, made him linger here when—

"I don't need you to tell me what's sensible."

"Well, someone certainly should. You're too stubborn."

"Me?" His tight control slipped. "I'm not the one coming up with crazy dreams for a town anyone can see is dying. Who put you in charge, you and your letters that won't make a bit of difference—" He stopped, seeing her pale. Muttering a curse, he dropped his head. Exhaled. "Look, I'm sorry."

Her blue eyes were wide and stricken, and he wished he could retract his bitter words. It wasn't Ivy's fault that he'd been gone when his brother had found his failures too much to bear. That his father might die without ever forgiving him. That he didn't know how to help Betsey without destroying Ivy's dream.

"It's not dying," she whispered. "I won't let it. I just have to figure out the right words to tell this man what a good thing he'd be doing."

"Ivy—" Linc plowed both hands through his

hair ''—you don't know what his situation is. You don't know anything about what this man might need or who he might owe or—'' He broke off, realizing he was dangerously close to revealing too much.

Ivy stood stock-still, her teeth worrying at that full lower lip that drove him wild.

Linc turned away. The last thing either of them needed was to add physical involvement to their wealth of problems.

''I hadn't thought of it that way,'' she said with wonder in her voice. ''You're right. I have to go there, to meet him and find out—''

''No—'' Linc spun back.

Ivy's eyes went wide.

He grasped for a reason. ''I mean, you can't go there unprepared. You should make a business plan.''

''What's that?''

He warmed to the idea. It would buy time. ''It's a blueprint for how much money you have in mind, how it would be spent, what the returns are. He's a businessman, Ivy. He has to think of the bottom line.''

She cocked her head. ''How do you know about things like that?''

Careful, Linc. He shrugged. ''I've worked a lot of places. I hear things. I…read a lot.''

New respect entered her gaze. "Could you show me how to prepare such a plan?"

Linc wanted to groan. He already knew it was hopeless, knew she was beaten before she started. Now he was going to help her get even more involved in this crazy scheme?

Then he realized that it was actually the answer he'd been seeking. He'd help Ivy with her business plan, and then she'd see that it was hopeless, that the numbers just didn't work. It was the least he could do.

"Will you come to the merchants' meeting tonight?" she asked.

"Merchants' meeting?"

She nodded. "The Greater Palo Verde Merchants' Association, which I've formed. I have to tell the others about this, and we have to compare notes on what you've been turning up. They'll want to do business plans, too."

Linc stifled a moan. He'd only meant to help Ivy out. He didn't have time to take care of a whole town.

But then he thought of Lora Lee and her grace in the face of so much loss. He remembered Howard and June Ledbetter, the auto mechanic and homemaker who'd retired and bet their savings on their antique store.

Damn. Why hadn't he considered before he

spoke? If he wasn't careful, Ivy would have him hopelessly embroiled in her half-baked scheme.

Then he looked at her, blue eyes bright with hope, and he couldn't summon the distance to tell her no. He'd have to be on his guard, but he'd negotiated multimillion-dollar projects. He could find a win-win situation in all this.

"All right," he said. "I'll come."

"Oh, thank you!" Ivy's face broke into a huge smile, and before he could react, she threw her arms around his neck and launched on tiptoes to kiss his cheek.

Except that he'd stumbled as her body collided with his, and the kiss missed its mark, landing on the corner of his mouth.

Without a moment's hesitation, Linc slanted his mouth over hers, tightening his arms around her waist and lifting her into his kiss.

The kiss might have begun in gratitude, but with shocking swiftness, everything changed. Ivy's gently rounded breasts against his chest, the new and sweet taste of her, shattered reason, and he wrapped her against him more tightly still.

Ivy gasped, then turned liquid in his arms. "Linc…" she murmured as she slid those long, delicate fingers into his hair.

It was lightning on dry timber. Linc could barely breathe, much less think. He'd known she was small and soft and kind…but there lay within the sweetness of Ivy Parker a passion beyond anything he would have dreamed.

Linc reveled in it, letting the shocking heat of it flash over him, stirring him to want more, to have her under him, to slide inside the rich lushness that was Ivy—

His conscience stirred. Demanded control.

She was a woman for a man who could love, a woman who gave heart's ease…a deep, inviting pool of warmth and comfort, a tender, generous soul who gave too much and asked nothing back.

And he was lying to her with every word. Even this stunning passion could not scorch away the taint of that.

So even though it pained him, with the feel of Ivy against him, her body trusting in his arms, Linc forced himself to slowly separate his aching body from her welcoming one.

Ivy breathed a tiny moan at the loss of contact. Her blue eyes drifted open—then, with a cry, she jerked away and wouldn't meet his gaze.

Linc felt like the world's biggest heel. "Ivy, it's not—"

"No." She waved him away, one hand pressed against those inviting lips.

"Ivy—"

She cut him off with a quick, vehement shake

of her still-bowed head. "Don't. I shouldn't have—"

"Ivy, you don't—" *Understand,* he thought. But how the hell could she?

Her back still to him, Ivy asked in a small voice, "Will you be coming to the meeting?"

Linc resisted the urge to slam his fist into a post. *What a tangled web we weave when first we practice to deceive....*

"Yes," he answered dully, then turned to go. "I'll see you there."

Ivy didn't speak; she merely nodded.

Linc waited for a moment but heard no other sound. Knowing she was waiting for him to leave, he did not what he wanted to do but what was the only right thing.

He left the kindest woman he'd ever met.

Alone. And better for it.

THAT NIGHT, Ivy topped off Silas McGee's coffee as around her, conversation swelled.

"You all right, Ivy?" the aged pillar of the square asked. Every day, rain or shine, he could be found walking the sidewalks or sitting under the trees on the courthouse lawn. He owned no building or business and was seldom found in the paint-weary, two-story house that had been his family home for a century. In many ways, though, Silas was the town crier of Palo Verde, the man who knew who had given birth and who had died—though the latter had exceeded the former for the past thirty years...one more marker that Palo Verde was dying.

A situation Ivy intended to correct.

"Where's that young fella been lookin' at all the buildings?" Silas asked.

Ivy had been working very hard at not thinking about Linc Garner, most especially about that... kiss. *Kiss* seemed too simple a word for what had transpired. She had been swirled up, drowned in bliss and dropped back to earth in the space of mere seconds.

If she lived to be a hundred, she didn't think she'd ever get over the humiliation of practically throwing herself into his arms. The punch of that kiss was no excuse.

Oh, he could kiss, all right. Heaven help her, the man could kiss. If he ever came to care for a woman, she'd be a lucky lady, indeed.

But Ivy would not be that woman; that much was clear. He'd looked at her with something she could only call pity, and had gently drawn away.

She'd had enough pity in her life, first as the ragtag foster child, the girl dressed in other people's hand-me-downs. She'd gone to four different high schools before she'd graduated, always a good workhorse but never a child to keep.

And then there was the pity she'd seen in the eyes of those who, it turned out, had known her husband had been cheating on her from the first. In the two women who'd shown up at his funeral, too much knowledge in their eyes.

And the neighbors who'd visited the hospital after she'd been unable to keep her baby within the shelter of her body. "Too bad," they'd said. "Poor thing."

She hated the word *pity* still.

She would not stand for it from Linc Garner. There was nothing she could do to banish his knowledge of how she'd abandoned herself in his arms, but she could make sure it never happened again—with anyone, but especially not with him.

If only she could forget how wonderful it had felt for those blissful moments before he'd stiffened and pulled away. He'd felt something, too, but it was only physical. Hadn't her husband told her a hundred times that men had needs? Linc was in a strange place, and she'd been available. Simple as that.

Well, she couldn't alter the image that he carried around inside his head, but she could change how she proceeded from here. Straightening her shoulders, Ivy focused on why this group of people had assembled, and she moved to the front of the room.

But when she turned to face them, the first person she saw was Linc, standing in back, leaning against the wall. For a charged second, his storm-cloud–gray eyes locked on hers.

Ivy jerked her gaze away. "All right," she said a little more loudly than usual. "Let's get down to business."

If only Linc would just vanish instead of standing there, taking up way too much of the air in the room. She closed her eyes for a second and tried to calm her nerves. "We're here tonight for the first meeting of the Palo Verde Merchants' Association. I've asked Lora Lee—" she pointed to the older woman, who was sitting erect and dignified at the table to Ivy's left "—to take the minutes. We should elect officers first, I think."

"Aw, Ivy, we don't need all that bureaucratic nonsense," Carl said. "Just declare yourself president, and we'll all back you—won't we, folks?"

She smiled. "You want me to declare myself dictator, Carl?"

"Won't be much different from the way you run the café," he grumbled. "Always telling me what and when to eat."

"If you had the sense God gave a goat, Carl Thompson, there'd be no need for Ivy to order you around," Aunt Prudie said. "You're too darn old to be so helpless."

"Helpless?" Carl exclaimed. "Who is it who's been letting Ivy do all the work just so you can lie around and play the queen of Sheba?"

Laughter rose. Prudie and Carl had been providing entertainment for the town for a long time.

"The queen was a harlot, you old goat. You bite that sharp tongue of yours before—"

"Excuse me, Aunt Prudie," Ivy said, glancing around the room, seeing amusement but also worry. "And Carl, shame on you for talking like that. Aunt Prudie's been very ill, and you know you've been worried sick about her."

Several loud chuckles erupted. Carl's face turned beet red. "Only worried she'll think she's well enough to start cooking again."

Aunt Prudie spluttered. "Why, you old coot, when I think of all the meals I cooked for you..." Her color heightened.

Ivy intervened. "All right, now. Aunt Prudie, settle yourself down. You're not fully recovered. And Carl, if you can't say something nice, don't—"

He folded his arms over his chest. "Don't say anything," he mimicked. "Too darn bossy for your own good, little girl."

"Carl—"

"Wouldn't know how to say something nice if your life depended on it," Aunt Prudie muttered.

"I'm going to send you both home if you can't behave." Ivy fought the urge to smile. She saw Linc's face creased in a grin, and she almost forgot where she'd been headed.

That grin was lethal.

Ivy blew out a breath that ruffled her bangs. "All right. Where were we?"

"Electing officers," Lora Lee said.

"Yes. Well, we're not a large group. Perhaps we could do without them?" Ivy asked the group.

June Ledbetter raised her hand. "I move that we elect Ivy our president and spokesperson. It's only fair, after all she's done."

"I haven't accomplished anything yet."

"But you will." June smiled.

"I don't know...I'm not getting anywhere with the landlord, but I promise I won't give up. Meantime, Mr. Garner has had a wonderful idea. He thinks we need to make a business plan, so that our landlord will know that we're serious and we know what we're asking."

"What's that mean?"

"It means—" Ivy halted. "Actually, Mr. Garner, perhaps it would be better if you explained what's involved."

Linc frowned and hesitated, but finally he

shoved away from the wall. "If you're going to convince this landlord to spend money fixing up these buildings, you need to show him what's in it for him. Show him some way he'll get his money back with a return to make it worth his while."

"How's that gonna happen?" Silas asked. "Nobody here's got any spare money."

"You can provide information, instead. Tourism statistics, cash flow projections, etcetera. You're going to have to demonstrate that it has value to him or he won't do it."

"Probably won't do it, anyway," Carl grumbled. "Fella don't have the decency to answer a letter."

Linc frowned. "Maybe he has reasons—"

"No good reason to be rude," Aunt Prudie retorted.

An odd look crossed Linc's face. He opened his mouth to speak, then didn't.

"I think Linc here should go with Ivy to Dallas, don't you folks?" Carl offered.

Stunned, Ivy shot a glance at Linc to see his response.

She didn't have to wait.

"No." Harsh. Emphatic. "That's not possible." A muscle in his jaw flexed.

Of course it wasn't. After she'd made a fool of herself, why would he want to be near her, much less stuck in a car all the way to Dallas for however long it took to find the landlord?

"Why not?" Howard asked. "You got someplace you got to be?" He cast a pointed look at Linc's worn clothing.

Linc flushed, but before he could speak, Ivy leaped to his defense. "Mr. Garner has done plenty for us, Howard. I'll remind you that he was hurt trying to help me, and he's been spending time on all your buildings with no pay for his effort. He's done more than enough to help us out."

Linc watched her, his face devoid of expression.

"That's exactly why he needs to go with you, girl," Carl said. "He's the one who understands what's required for the buildings. You cook like an angel, but you don't know squat about construction. He's the one who came up with this business plan idea, too."

Ivy tried to marshal an argument aside from the one most telling—and most humiliating: that Linc Garner wouldn't want to be alone with her. "But—"

Finally, Linc spoke. "All that's true, Carl, but I can write it up for her to present. What man in his right mind would want to talk to me when he could talk to a beautiful blonde?"

Laughter erupted, dispersing the tension.

But Ivy burned. He could make light of it all he

wanted, but she knew the compliments were just words. He didn't think she was beautiful, only pitiful. Man-hungry or something equally pathetic.

"Well, you got yourself a point there, Linc," Howard said. "Still, we'd all be beholden to you if you'd reconsider." He looked around the room. "We can't scrape up too much among us, but we could make it worth your while in other ways. I'd be willing to donate work on your truck, and I bet Charlie would stand you to a new change of clothes. Together, we could barter goods for your time, and we'd be mighty grateful if you'd help our Ivy here make her case."

Linc looked so uncomfortable that Ivy squirmed. If a man so down on his luck could reject the offer, he must really not want to be stuck spending time with her. "Please. Don't badger Linc. He's done enough for all of us. It's not our right to pry into his plans or to make him feel obliged. We can take care of ourselves," she said. "He's armed us with information, and that's already worth everything you've offered, Howard. I think he deserves all that without doing one thing more."

She saw chagrin on some faces, nods of agreement on others. Linc's face had gone hard and stiff, his jaw clenched. For a man of such pride, the discussion had to be misery.

She glanced at the clock. "It's getting late—past my bedtime," she joked.

"Wasn't aware you ever slept, girl," Carl said. For once, he and Prudie were in agreement. "You're right about that," her aunt said.

Ivy had suffered about all the discomfort she could stand for one night, but she plastered a smile on her face. "Be that as it may, I think we have the beginnings of a plan. Anyone who wants to pitch in, perhaps we could work on it tomorrow afternoon after I close up."

People were already rising and talking to one another. "I want to be in Dallas within the next week," she said, lifting her voice. "I'll keep you all posted. Anyone who would like to go with me is more than welcome."

As the gathering broke up, Linc moved to her side. "Ivy, it's not that I—"

She shook her head, not wanting to have this discussion within earshot of her neighbors. "It's not necessary to explain," she said, focusing on the papers in her hand. "We've presumed upon you more than enough." She lifted her gaze to his but averted it quickly. "I need to let everyone out." She turned away. "Good night, Linc."

He grasped her arm. "Ivy—"

"I need to go now," she repeated, hoping he couldn't feel her tremble. "Please."

He let her go. "We have to talk, Ivy."

Not now, was all she could think. *Not ever.* But just then, Carl approached and saved her from having to answer.

LINC TOSSED BACK the covers and gave up. He couldn't sleep; every time he tried to close his eyes, he saw the hurt in Ivy's still, solemn face. She'd had to have misunderstood his reason for ending the kiss, and he wanted to set her straight—except that this was exactly what he needed: distance. A reason for her to be glad he would leave. He had no business getting any more involved in Ivy's life; his great plan had backfired in a wholly unexpected way. Of all the outcomes he'd expected when meeting the crackpot blue-haired Ivy Parker, he'd never even considered that he'd one day wind up kissing her…and wanting more.

Just then, he heard a noise from downstairs in the café. With rapid moves he donned the jeans he'd left lying on the floor and slid his feet into his shoes. The first thing he would do when he got home to Denver was burn these clothes—if he never saw any of them again, it would be too soon.

In the kitchen, he grabbed a knife to arm himself against a possible intruder. With careful steps he crossed the floor, wondering if someone was after the cash register—

Then he heard her voice.

A moment later, he saw her. Ivy...in that same should-have-been-demure white cotton nightgown, her long locks falling gloriously around her shoulders—

Standing on tiptoe on a stepladder, stripping wallpaper with only one faint light to guide her. And humming.

"What are you doing?" he asked.

Startled, she turned too fast and slipped. Linc leaped forward to arrest her fall, but she caught herself first.

"What does it look like?" she asked in a listless tone.

"Ivy, *do* you ever sleep?"

She sighed, shoulders drooping. "Don't, Linc. I don't need anyone else clucking over me."

"Bull. You need a keeper. You can't keep going this way. No one can."

Ivy straightened and sprayed the wallpaper again. Then she picked up the scraper. "I have to," she murmured. "There's no one else."

"Ivy, towns die all the time. You can't—"

She grabbed the ladder and whirled to face him. "This one won't. Do you hear me, Linc Garner? I won't let it." She was a Valkyrie, her golden hair a nimbus around a face shining with purpose.

God, she was magnificent. And headed straight

for failure. He made a mental note to call Maggie first thing and light a fire under the efforts to find Ivy a new location.

That settled in his mind, he walked to the wall beside her, keeping a careful distance between them.

"What are you doing?" she asked.

He peeled at one edge of the paper. "Lending a hand so you'll go get some sleep."

"Linc, you can't—"

"Hush, Ivy. Just once, let someone help."

Her eyes were huge and stricken. "You've already done too much."

She had that right, but not in the way she thought. "Ivy, I'll come to the meeting tomorrow, but then I have to go." Betsey's last update had made it clear he shouldn't linger, and he had enough information now—too much for his peace of mind. He needed to get away from the lure of Ivy and back to his real life.

Even if there was something soothing and peaceful about stripping wallpaper with her in this faint, intimate circle of golden light.

"Is it anything I could help with?" she asked.

How like her to offer. "No."

Ivy was silent for a moment. "Where's your family, Linc?"

"Only my father is left. My brother died six

months ago. My mother's been gone since I was a kid.''

"I'm sorry," she said. "My parents are dead, too." Voice soft as if in a confessional, she spoke again. "I have two sisters, but I haven't seen either of them since we were kids."

Was this the sorrow he'd seen in her eyes? "What happened?"

She shrugged. "After my mother died, there was no one else."

"What about Prudie? Isn't she really your aunt?"

"Great-aunt." Ivy glanced up. "It's not her fault. She didn't know. Her husband was a sailor, so they were always traveling. My father was estranged from his family, so we weren't often in touch. I'd only met her once."

Only once, but she'd given up her life and home to come take care of a woman she barely knew? Linc shook his head. He didn't need to ask. He'd seen Ivy's penchant for taking in strays and lost souls. "So what happened to your sisters?"

Ivy stiffened and pain washed over her face. She hesitated so long, he wasn't sure she would answer.

"Forget it," he said, placing one hand on her arm. "It's not my business."

She turned to him, eyes filled with tears. "It's

just—my little sister Chloe was adopted. I don't know what happened to Caroline after she ran away from foster care."

"You were separated?"

"No one wanted two teenagers and a pre-schooler. I tried to be good so they'd see I could help and we wouldn't be any trouble, but—" Ivy blinked rapidly and began ripping paper with a vengeance.

Linc wanted to ask why she hadn't searched for them, but maybe she had. He knew better than most how easy it was to disappear. Anyway, it wasn't his business.

But he still couldn't let the subject go. Not when he could see that she hurt so badly. He closed the distance between them and lifted her from her perch on the ladder, folding her into his arms. She stiffened against him, but he kept his hold gentle, trying to make it clear that this was about comfort, not about sex. Stroking her hair, he pried open his own heart a crack. "I understand how it hurts. I've been gone from my family for fifteen years."

When she tilted her head back, her eyes asking why, Linc shrugged. "It's a long story. Just let me hold you, instead."

He tried to pull her head against him again to escape those too-soft, too-aware blue eyes. Ivy resisted, lifting one hand to his face. "I'm sorry, Linc."

The touch of her hand was a benediction on a world-weary soul. For an endless moment, Linc let himself soak in her kindness, her generous heart. Peace washed over him, filling in raw, dark holes. Though he wanted to kiss her, wanted to make love to her in the worst way, he had a sense of something else he craved, something beyond the physical.

But he wasn't free to have it. With regret, he drew away. Looked anywhere else but at her sweet face. "Ivy, I don't want to make you think I can—"

She jumped back, face flaming. "I—I think I'll go to bed now. This job will take a few days, anyway."

He felt like scum. "Ivy, it's not—" The words died in his throat.

She paused in the doorway. Linc wanted to explain that it wasn't her fault. He'd meant to comfort her, but he'd caused her more hurt. It was the last thing he wanted. Loathing himself and his predicament, he remained silent.

Her voice shaking, Ivy spoke. "Just leave everything. I'll clean it up in the morning." And then she was gone.

Linc swore, watching her go. He stood there for

a moment, wondering how this could get any worse.

Then he grabbed the spray bottle and scraper and went to work.

CHAPTER EIGHT

IVY PICKED HER WAY across the dew-sparkled grass, listening to the mockingbird singing nearby. Dawn the pale inner pink of a seashell lit her way as she breathed in the sweet scent of honeysuckle. The world felt fresh and new, and it lifted her heart.

She cast a glance toward Linc's bedroom window and the glow dimmed.

She'd slept surprisingly well after their late-night encounter; she hadn't expected to sleep at all. Not after making a fool of herself once again. Hadn't she learned long ago that she was not someone people wanted to keep? Even a down-on-his-luck handyman was ready to be on his way.

If only she hadn't felt such safety in his arms. For a sparkling instant, shelter had wrapped itself around her and tantalized her with a glimpse of what she'd sought for years: a man's strong arms. A heart to care for. Someone on whom she could, at long last, lean…and feel safe.

Oh, go on with you, Ivy. He wasn't rude or cruel about turning away from you.

That was true, and it made the situation all the more embarrassing. He'd offered simple friendship, and her hungry heart had reached for more. She'd wanted to nestle in those strong arms and never leave. Wanted to wrap herself around him like her namesake and sink in roots that would keep him here.

She reached for the handle of the screen door at the back of the café and shook her head. She'd built a mountain out of a molehill…or perhaps only a grain of sand. A stranger had offered simple kindness, and she'd weakened.

What was it about Linc Garner that toppled all her carefully constructed walls? She'd thought she had reconciled herself to a life with this odd little family, to holding other women's babies and feeding strangers and friends. She'd lost two families and she was bound and determined to hold this one—such as it was—together, no matter what.

Then into her life walked a man who made her want all those old dreams again. Bittersweet, painful dreams she'd consigned to the musty attic of a girl's far-off past.

Well, what was done was done. Nothing to do now but go on. She could use Linc's help on the business plan, but she wouldn't keep him a second longer than she must in order to understand what was needed. Then she would wish him well and send him on his way to wherever he'd been headed when he had the poor judgment to stop at her café and ask for work.

Tying the apron around her waist, Ivy headed into the next room to clean up the mess she'd left unfinished—

Only there was no mess. And no wallpaper. The walls were stripped and prepped, ready for covering again. The ladder had been put away, the scraps cleaned up, the floor left spotless.

Ivy stared, one hand over her mouth. If she'd been given diamonds, it couldn't have meant more. No one had ever done anything like this for her, not ever.

Just once, let someone help.

Oh, Linc…

Ivy studied the walls for a long time, her throat crowded, her heart full.

Then she stirred as if from a dream, forced herself back to reality.

And work. Thank goodness for work.

LINC RUBBED GRITTY EYES and listened to the phone ring and ring. Betsey wouldn't be awake yet—mornings were not her thing. Not like Ivy, who awoke with cheer already bright in her eyes.

Ivy, whom he'd hurt. Again.

Though he was trying to do the right thing, he seemed to always do the reverse. He'd had only an hour's sleep last night, but it had been worth it. Ivy hadn't let him do any repairs for her; he'd taken pleasure, tired or not, in doing that one job for her. In taking one burden off her too-weighted shoulders.

And working with his hands again had felt good. Once that had been his livelihood; he hadn't realized how he'd missed it. His world had been simpler when he'd lived in jeans and out of his truck. Then suits and fancy dinners had taken over.

"Hello?" a sleepy voice answered.

"Hi, Bets."

"Linc—" Pleasure suffused her voice. He heard the sound of sheets rustling. What did Betsey wear to bed? For years, he'd tortured himself wondering about that. Picturing her in the arms of his brother. "Are you home?" she asked.

No. *Yes.* "No," he answered. "I just—" Wanted to touch base with the real world. Needed to remember why he'd come.

"I'm glad you called," she said, and he could hear it in her voice.

"Even if I woke you up?" A slow grin crossed his face. Yeah. This was what he'd needed.

"Even if." Her voice was shy and a little husky.

Linc let himself imagine her...what she wore, the color of her sheets—

But all he could see was white cotton and long blond curls....

"Linc?"

The image vanished, a heart's wish replaced by what could be. What could matter.

He sat up straight, ignoring the ache of it. "I— I'll be home tomorrow, Bets. How's—" *Dad.* As a kid, he'd wished for the kind of father a boy could call Dad, but his father had never been one for something so casual. "How's he doing?"

"I'm glad you're coming. He's...agitated. He seems to feel an urgency about talking to you."

"Should I phone him?"

"No. I offered that, but he wants to see you, he says."

"Of course." Just like the old man. Always had to call the shots. Always on his terms.

"Linc, he's—" She paused. "I know he wasn't the best father."

Understatement of the year, Linc thought. But didn't say it.

"But I think he really regrets all the years you and he have lost. Now that Garner's gone, you two only have each other. Can't you forgive him, Linc?"

"Me? He's the one who refuses—" His father

had made it clear to him years ago that his sins were too black. That any chance for forgiveness and being brought back into the fold was more distant than the farthest star. Fury kindled. "I didn't do—" *Anything wrong,* he'd started to say.

But he had. Over and over again. That the moves were those of a boy desperate for his father's attention, however it had to be gained, didn't matter. The mature man now saw what the boy had been too angry and hungry to see: Edward Lincoln Galloway II could not be the type of father Linc needed. It didn't matter why; it just was.

"I can't talk about it now, Bets. I—" He closed his eyes. "Let him know I'll be there tomorrow."

"He asked me not to tell you this, Linc, but you need to hurry. He wanted you to come of your own accord, not because you felt sorry for him. Not because he was..."

Dying. That was what she meant. "He's so much worse? Why didn't somebody speak up?"

"You can't reveal that you know. Give him that much, at least."

"How long does he have?"

"A week, maybe two. The doctors aren't sure. I'm taking him home. He wants to die in his own bed."

Linc glanced across the trees but saw nothing. His father was really dying. All that had been unresolved for years would remain that way unless he—

"Oh, Bets..." He sank back into the seat, bone tired.

"I'm sorry, Linc. You've lost so much."

He heard the tears in her voice. "So have you."

"I need you," she whispered. "Please come."

He shoved away useless wishes. Here was duty. Here was honor. "We'll get through this, Bets. I'll finish up and leave today if I can." His promise to Ivy hung heavy on his head, but a promise was a promise. He'd outline what had to be done for the business plan, but he wouldn't stay to walk her through it. He'd come back later, when his father—

Images assaulted him: big, healthy, imperious male; frail and frightened old man; his father in all his seasons and faces.

He'd think of that later. He had too much to do right now.

"Keep Maggie posted," he said. "I'll check in as often as possible." He was tempted to say to hell with it and simply carry his cell phone with him. But one image of the hurt in Ivy's soft blue eyes stopped him.

There wasn't much left he could do for her, but this was not the time to tell her who he really was and hurt her more. Later, he'd—

He couldn't think about later. Too much to be done now. "Take care of yourself, Betsey," he said. "I'll see you soon." He punched the off button and started the truck, then made a U turn and headed back.

"OLD MAN, you don't know what you're talking about," Aunt Prudie spluttered.

Carl sat in his usual booth, but his coffee had gone untasted. "Shows what you know. I'm telling you Ivy needs that boy. Deserves a good man like him."

Prudie nodded with sorrow. "I can't disagree about that. Best thing could happen to her is that he'd sweep her up and take her away with him. But it's not going to happen."

Carl scowled without his usual fervor. "Why not? Girl ain't stupid. Surely she can see he's a good one."

Prudie shook her head. "It doesn't matter. Ivy's made up her mind not to fall in love again. She's lost too much."

Carl leaned closer. "What's that mean?"

Ivy hadn't meant to eavesdrop. Hadn't wanted to interrupt, but they were treading dangerous ground. "Aunt Prudie, could you help me, please?"

Her great-aunt jerked as if caught with one hand in the cookie jar. "Sure thing, hon. What do you need?"

"Lora Lee and I are working on a description

of our idea, but the coffee's getting low. Would it be too much trouble for you to make more?"

Aunt Prudie rose, her back straightening. "Don't imagine I've forgotten how to make coffee in my own café."

Ivy resisted the urge to grin. "I'm sure you haven't. After all, you taught me everything I know."

Her aunt harrumphed, then moved toward the kitchen with slow steps, leaning on her cane.

Ivy bit her lip, wondering if she'd asked too much.

"She'll be fine," Carl said. "Woman that thick-headed is darn near impossible to keep down. 'Sides, does a body good to feel useful." He sighed and leaned his head back.

"You're not eating. Are you all right, Carl?"

He straightened. "Just a little weary. Happens when you get old."

Ivy scanned him with a worried glance. His color didn't look good. "Carl, I didn't mean to hurt you, letting Linc help out."

The older man shrugged. "Facts is facts, girl. Boy's younger and stronger. It's the way of the world."

She heard the hurt in his tone, though, and slid into the booth across from him, reaching for his gnarled hand. "He can never replace what you mean to me, Carl. You're my friend, and I count on you. You've been there to help me every step of the way, and I'll never be able to repay you.''

His ancient, weathered cheeks had gone pink, his eyes suspiciously bright. ''Get on with you, girl. You'd have done it all just fine by yourself.''

She tightened her grip as her throat crowded. ''That's not true.'' Her voice quavered. ''I honestly don't know what I'd have done without you these past months.''

He shrugged and glanced away, but she could see the pride. ''Glad if I could help you, Ivy girl, but that boy's what you need.''

Sorrow dimmed the bright morning. ''No,'' she whispered. ''He's not.'' He wouldn't stay. And if she wished otherwise—

Well, it couldn't matter. Ivy stood and rounded the table, leaning down to hug the old man who'd become the father she'd lost so long ago. He was real, and he would stay here. People like him were why she wanted to make this town live again, so Carl's grandchildren—and their grandchildren— wouldn't have to move away.

''You're the only man in my life, Carl. And that's just fine with me.'' She pressed a kiss to his cheek, then started to turn away.

His voice stopped her. ''Don't you give up on love, Ivy girl. Woman like you is meant to fill a home with it. To make strong, healthy babies and love one man all her life.''

His intentions were good, she knew, but it was

all she could do to stand there and not run. Her whole body trembled with her need to escape from a yearning so strong it was a physical hunger. Carl had put voice to her deepest dream—and she knew it would never happen.

Just then the front door creaked open, and in walked Linc.

Ivy could have been turned to stone, except stone didn't breathe. Stone didn't ache. Stone didn't hunger, and stone didn't need.

His gaze scanned the room, then landed on her like a blow to the stomach. A punch to the heart.

Ivy swiveled, seeking escape. Yearning for a place to gather her wits and get ready to talk business and only business with the man who made her want so much...too much that she knew in her depths she would never have. His eyes assured her of that. His expression said he was impatient to leave. Was already half gone.

But Ivy Parker was no coward, so instead of running away, she smiled at him, hoping her smile was that of a hostess. Quick and impersonal. Just enough to get the job done.

She still needed information from him, but she would obtain it quickly, feed him one last meal in repayment, and watch as he drove away, his work done.

"Hello, Linc." She grabbed her pot of now-lukewarm coffee and strode toward him. "Aunt

Prudie's making more coffee in the kitchen. Have you eaten?"

He didn't respond, but only stared at her in a manner she couldn't read. Just as she was ready to turn away, he broke his silence.

"I have to leave soon." His tone was flat, impartial.

Ivy swallowed her hurt. "Perhaps you can outline what's required on the business plan while you eat. If you'll excuse me, I'll get your plate ready." She began to turn.

"No." He grasped her free wrist and stopped her.

She couldn't bring herself to look at him again. "Fine. If you don't have time to tell me, I still want to feed you a meal. It's poor repayment for all the work you did last night, but—"

As she tried to free herself from his grip, though, his hand only tightened, to the point that she wanted to cry out.

As if she had, he suddenly let go. "I'm sorry," he muttered in a harsh voice. "Ivy, you don't owe me anything. I wish I could—" He stopped, shook his head. "It's not that I want to go." A soft curse erupted from his lips. He glanced away, and Ivy saw something dark and sad cross his features.

Then, before her eyes, he became someone else, someone cold and formidable, more contained than ever. All traces of warmth and regret, if that was what they had been, fled.

When he turned to her again, he seemed a different person from the man who'd captivated her so. "No food, but a cup of coffee would be nice. Then I'll outline what's needed before I leave."

Ivy stared at him for a moment longer, wishing they were alone and she had the right to pry.

But she didn't have the right. Everything about him said *Hands off.* And in a strange way, his very reserve settled her. Brought her back to herself, the woman who didn't need to lean.

"Fine. I'll be back with fresh coffee and a pen and paper."

She walked away, hoping the shaking in her legs would not betray her.

LINC WATCHED HER GO and again felt like the lowest scum on the earth. This wasn't how he wanted to leave her, but perhaps it was for the best. Their lives were separate and always would be. Betsey needed him. Ivy would be fine on her own.

But even as he thought that, he remembered her curling against him with such trust last night, if so briefly, and wondered again what drove Ivy to take care of everyone else but to allow no one to care for her.

Ivy reentered the room with Stevie on one arm and a pot of fresh coffee in her free hand.

"Don't tell me you're baby-sitting again," Carl grumbled.

"Okay, I won't." Her tone tart, she set down

the pot and turned over a mug for Linc. The little girl dove toward the colorful mat under the hot pot.

Linc reached for her, but Ivy's reflexes were quicker. Grasping Stevie tightly, she whirled away. "Could you pour your own coffee, please, Linc?" Her voice shook slightly. "Let me settle the baby, and I'll be right back."

Linc watched her walk away, stroking the little girl's hair, pressing Stevie into the curve of her neck. With deft moves, she spread a quilt in the corner and placed the child on it with a basket of brightly colored toys. Ivy played with her for a minute, and Linc saw her face smooth out, glowing with joy. Why she had no children of her own he'd never understand. Surely fate would not have been so unkind as to make her unable to bear her own. Caught by the thought, Linc wondered if Ivy's sadness stemmed from more than the husband and sisters she had lost.

If ever there was a woman meant to be loved and cherished in a family of her own, Ivy Parker was that woman.

To realize he wished he could be that woman's man shocked him.

He spun around and filled his cup.

Carl caught his gaze. "You headed out so soon, boy? What's your rush?"

Linc shrugged. His reasons must remain his own. "It's time."

A muffled curse escaped Carl's lips. "You

gonna just go off and leave that little gal with all this on her shoulders?''

Linc leveled the look on him that had felled corporate presidents and brought contractors to heel. ''My plans are none of your business.''

If he thought this bandy-legged old man would be intimidated, he thought wrong.

''How can you do it, boy?'' Carl rasped. ''Can't you see she needs you?''

Those who'd done business with Linc would have laughed at the idea that a man a foot shorter and forty years older than Linc could make him quail, but Linc wasn't laughing.

''Carl, I wish I could help her, but—''

The older man's furious gaze slid away. Linc caught Ivy's cinnamon-and-flowers scent before he heard her.

''Carl?'' Her brows lifted. ''Is something wrong?''

Carl shot Linc a warning glance. Linc didn't flinch.

''Guess not.'' With effort, the old man came to his feet, then walked away as if from a leper.

Watching him go, Linc sipped the coffee too quickly and burned his tongue. He set down the cup with a *bang,* sloshing hot coffee over the side, splashing his shirt. Swearing, he leaped up.

''I'm sorry. I'll get a rag.'' Ivy headed for the kitchen.

"Why are you sorry? I'm the one who—" But she was gone.

He followed her. "Ivy, damn it, I—"

Inside the kitchen, he stopped. Ivy stood by the sink with her back to him, slender shoulders rounded.

And shaking.

Linc cursed fate and timing and the luck that hadn't failed him in years. He'd hurt her again, damn it. "Ivy—" He reached for her.

She eluded his grasp. He had to confront the fact that he was not the comfort she wanted. That he couldn't stay around to change that.

Just then, they heard a scream and shattering glass. A heavy *thud*. A child's terrified wail.

Linc charged through the doorway. For a moment, he couldn't tell what had happened past the jumble of overturned chairs and Stevie's screaming.

Ivy shot past him and grabbed the little girl. Beside her on the floor lay the coffee carafe, smashed, the tablecloth stained and dragging. Something behind the table—

Carl. Struggling to rise. Falling backward with a groan.

"Carl!" Ivy cried.

Linc raced to the old man's side, seeing his face drained of all color, the hand pressed to his chest. Linc had had a foreman suffer a heart attack once. This looked familiar.

"Lie still," he ordered, loosening the collar of Carl's shirt, yelling over his shoulder, "Ivy, call for help."

"I'll do it." Lora Lee had the phone in her hand, already punching in numbers.

"Baby's trying to pull up—" Carl gasped. "Chest—hurts—"

Prudie spoke then, her voice quavering. "Don't talk, Carl. Just lie still."

Ivy dropped to her knees beside Carl, movements jerky as she tried to soothe the screaming baby in her arms. "Oh, Linc, what is it? Carl—"

Linc spared one glance at her. "Easy. Everybody stay calm." He could hear his own blood rushing, pounding in his ears.

"Linc," Lora Lee shouted from behind the counter, "they said fifteen minutes. He's conscious and breathing, right?"

"Yes." Those were good signs, but he'd learned before how critical time was.

"They want to know if he's in pain and where."

"His chest," Linc replied, watching Carl's face. "What about your arms?"

Carl nodded.

"Left arm worse?"

One quick nod.

"They want to know what it feels like."

Linc gripped Carl's hand, seeing sweat bead on his forehead. "Can you tell me?"

"Fist—" Carl gasped. "Squeeze—hard—"

"Any history of heart problems?"

Carl shook his head.

Linc relayed it.

Lora Lee spoke again. "Taking any medications?"

Carl choked out names. Linc heard Lora Lee passing them along.

"Ivy," Lora Lee yelled, "they want him to chew up an aspirin. Do you have any?"

"I'll get one." Ivy jumped to her feet, her arms tight around the child whose screams had died into sobs. She darted into the kitchen.

"They want a pulse, Linc."

He placed two fingers on Carl's carotid artery, turning his own wrist so he could see the sweep hand on his watch. "Pulse about ninety-five and irregular."

Ivy dropped beside Carl again, her eyes skittering as fast as Carl's heartbeat. Linc saw her hands tremble and grabbed the bottle. He opened it, shook out one aspirin and placed it in Carl's mouth.

"Prudie, some water, please." He turned to Lora Lee. "He can have water?"

She spoke into the phone, then nodded. "Yes, but only a little."

"I'll get it," Ivy said.

"No. Let Prudie go," Linc ordered. Ivy looked as if someone had beaten her up. Pale and pinched...and stricken to her soul.

Carl needed calm. "Tell me how the baby is," Linc urged.

"What?" Ivy's ravaged eyes lifted. "She's—she's fine. Just scared." Her gaze dropped. "I left that carafe on the table," she whispered. "Oh, Carl—" Her voice broke.

"Let me take her," Linc said. He eased the baby from Ivy's arms. Ivy curled her body over Carl's as though she could protect him from the pain. Linc stroked one hand over her bright hair, wishing he could give her assurances no one could know yet. "It wasn't your fault."

"Boy's—right—" Carl's face was whiter than the tablecloths, the bones of his face standing out as he fought the pain. "Tell—old woman—" Each word came out with effort.

Ivy frowned. "Aunt Prudie?"

Carl nodded faintly. "Not—rid—me—yet." His eyes squeezed shut in agony.

"Hush, you old goat." Prudie appeared beside them, glass of water in her hand. Worry clouded her eyes. "You gonna try to make me get down on the floor with you, after all these years?" She shook her gunmetal curls. "I think not." But despite her words, she began to kneel.

Linc assisted her, moving aside to make room.

Prudie cradled Carl's head in one hand, holding the cup to his lips. "Hear that siren? They're on their way."

Linc glanced at Ivy, but she only had eyes for

Carl. He edged away from the intimate tableau, an outsider again. Baby held close, he rose to go outside and direct the paramedics. The child's sobs died to stuttery sniffles. She laid her head against his neck, her whole body going boneless, and something inside Linc ached.

"Come on, little girl," he murmured. "We're only in the way now."

CHAPTER NINE

LINC CURSED the slow pickup, banging the heel of
his hand on the steering wheel as the truck refused
to budge above fifty miles an hour. The landscape
crawled by as he headed for the hospital where
they'd taken Carl; his mind was focused on his last
glimpse of Ivy's haunted face as she'd climbed
into the ambulance.

Despair had shadowed her features and drawn
her skin taut across her bones. Even as scared as
she was, she'd still had the forethought to have
Lora Lee call Sally and to clasp Prudie to her
briefly, whispering words of comfort.

How like her to think of everyone else, when
Linc knew that she was dying inside, donning a
hair shirt of guilt for something that had been an
accident. She was only human, for God's sake, but
Ivy never seemed to allow herself any failings. He
was beginning to see that beneath her warm maternal air she was as driven as anyone he'd ever
met—even himself. She deceived with her flowered dresses and ponytail, but no drill sergeant

could be as exacting—except in Ivy's case, she only had those superhuman expectations of herself. Ninety-eight percent wasn't good enough. Only perfection counted. She made allowances for everyone else. Reserved no emotional space between herself and those for whom she cared.

If only she cared half as much for Ivy. She never did a damn thing to protect that tender heart.

He hit the redial button on his cell phone again, then swore as he realized he was still out of range. He needed to make Betsey aware that he'd be delayed. No matter what he'd promised her, he couldn't leave Ivy now—not until he was sure she would be all right. If he was a praying man, he'd pray for Carl. He didn't know how Ivy would handle it if anything happened to the old man.

As he pulled into Mineral Wells, he attempted the phone call again. Betsey answered.

"Betsey, I'll still try to leave today, but there's been an accident, and I have to stay until I see how things are."

"Are you okay?"

"Yeah. It's not me—it's Carl. He's been hurt and Ivy's scared."

"Who's Carl? Who's Ivy? Why does she need you?"

The hospital appeared before him. Linc's sense

of urgency rocketed. "I can't explain now—I'm at the hospital. I'll be in touch."

Just as he was about to disconnect, her voice stopped him. "Linc, are you sure you're all right?"

A simple question with no answer in sight. "I don't know." Linc sighed, suddenly weary. "I'll talk to you later, Bets."

"Come back home, Linc," she said. "I'm worried about you."

"I'll be fine. Don't fret about me. 'Bye, Bets." He hit the button to end the call, his mind caught by her words.

Home. Where was that, really? He didn't honestly know. He'd never let himself think about it, not since the day he'd been thrust out into the world alone. It had seemed irrelevant; he'd been focused on showing his father what a big mistake the older man had made.

Home. It shocked him to his toes to realize the only place that warranted the name bore the features of a small, soft, sweet woman trying to save a dusty, dying town.

And he was destined to betray them both.

HE FOUND IVY standing outside the emergency waiting room, staring down the hall as if she could will someone to appear. She still wore her apron, but there was little else left of the vivacious woman he'd come to expect to see.

This Ivy had withdrawn into herself. For as long as he'd known her, she'd always exuded warmth, but now she was as cold as if night had descended on her heart. Her arms were wrapped around her waist as though she were holding herself together by force.

"Ivy," he said, but she didn't answer. He called her name a second time, and she turned to him, her face bloodless, her eyes drained of all life. He wanted to reach out to her and enfold her in his arms, but he had no right. Stuffing his hands into his pockets, he asked, "How is he?"

She looked through him as if he hadn't spoken. Her pallor alarmed him. Maybe something had happened—

He grasped her arm. "Where is Carl? Is he—?"

She glanced down at his hand as though she didn't recognize what it was. Slowly, she returned her gaze to him, but he still couldn't make out a flicker of life.

"Ivy, talk to me." He swore, then glanced around, assessing where to go to find answers. "Never mind—"

Finally, she spoke, her voice as lifeless as her eyes. "I don't know. They took him in. They won't let me—'' Her voice wavered as she looked back down the hall.

He started in that direction to get some information, but a glance back had him swearing again. He didn't want to leave her alone for a second, yet he knew she needed answers. He retraced his steps and clasped her shoulders. She trembled like a leaf caught in winter's first icy wind.

He pulled her into his arms. She came like a wooden doll.

He tightened his arms around her and pressed a kiss to her hair, his heart suddenly too full, too embroiled in emotions he didn't know how to handle.

So he just held on.

Her trembling increased, but she didn't make a sound.

''Ivy,'' he said into her hair. ''I don't want to leave you.'' As he uttered the words, he realized they meant more than simply leaving her long enough to ask some questions.

He'd have to think about that later.

Stroking her hair, he rocked her gently from side to side. ''Sweetheart, he's a tough old guy. He'll be okay.'' He hoped to God he was right. Murmuring nonsense words and soothing phrases, he rubbed one hand up and down her back, wishing she'd say something, anything, to let him know he was getting through to her, but it was as though her soul had fled.

Maybe some news would help. With reluctance, he drew away. "I'm going to check with the staff. Sit down over here, and I'll be right back, okay?"

She didn't answer, only retreated from his embrace and stood there, looking alone and forlorn.

It was all he could do to leave her, but in case the news wasn't good, he wanted time to think how to tell her. He eased her into a chair in the waiting room. She went without comment or reaction. "I'll hurry, I promise."

This was one promise he could make to her and know he would be able to deliver. Glancing back twice before he reached the nurses' desk, he checked to make sure she was all right—and clenched his jaw when he saw her perched stiffly, her back not touching the chair.

He couldn't find out much, but he understood better why she was so scared. Carl had lost consciousness on the ambulance ride, which must have terrified Ivy. The nurses could only assure Linc that Carl had plenty of people working on him and that someone would be out to talk to them as soon as news was available.

When he returned, she was sitting with white-knuckled hands gripped together in her lap. He crouched in front of her and placed his hands over hers. "Ivy?"

Her gaze lifted to his, and he saw the first flicker of hope. "I'm sorry. They don't know anything yet." To watch that flicker die hurt. He wanted to find some way to bring her out from wherever she'd gone. "They told me his heart stopped and he lost consciousness. I know it must have scared you."

Her blue eyes wavered briefly. Then nothing.

"Listen, they said it's important that he was in the care of paramedics...that they got the heart restarted immediately and had him on oxygen." He felt the trembling begin again and slid his hands up her arms to clasp her shoulders. "Ivy, it wasn't your fault. Accidents happen."

She blinked, and for a second, she was back with him. "Stevie?" Her voice was barely a whisper.

"You were right. She's fine, just frightened. Sally came to get her."

The only sign that she'd heard him was a nod so faint he wasn't sure he hadn't imagined it.

"Carl will be fine, too." He offered reassurances he had no right to make.

It didn't matter. She showed no response.

Linc shot to his feet, wanting something to do, some way to make it right. Some way to bring back the Ivy he'd come to count on for her irrepressible cheer, her sturdy competence, her unstinting will.

"I'll get you some coffee, all right?" When she didn't answer, he stood there for a second, torn by his sense that he was failing two different women, both of whom needed him now. Exhaling sharply, he went searching for coffee.

He checked with the nurses again on his way back, but still no news. Taking a seat on the scarred plastic chair beside her, he handed one cup to Ivy. She took it but made no effort to drink.

"I didn't know how you like it. I mean, you remember how everyone drinks their coffee, but I've never seen you stop long enough to drink any." He frowned, realizing he was close to babbling. "Do you even like coffee?"

Nothing. Exasperation took over. "Damn it, Ivy, you can't do Carl any good like this. He's going to be all right." *He has to be.* Linc turned away, his guilt and rage mingling with a sense of helplessness he'd not felt in years.

People died. Carl was old. Ivy surely knew what Linc didn't want to admit, though he was intimately aware just how many things could go wrong in life, despite anyone's good intentions.

Linc closed his eyes and forced a deep, calming breath. He was here for Ivy. What he needed, what he wanted, what he felt weren't important. And nothing he could say or do would make a difference. It was all in the hands of the doctors now.

He settled back into the chair to wait beside the fragile, too-still woman who'd somehow, without warning, become far too important to him.

FINALLY, SOMEONE APPROACHED. Linc jumped to his feet. Ivy rose, still gripping the now-cold coffee. Linc eased it from her icy fingers and set it down, then slid one arm around her stiff shoulders.

"Are you Mr. Thompson's family?" the doctor asked.

Ivy remained in her shell, her body brittle and cold.

Linc spoke up. "We're all the family he has." Though the irony of that struck him, he didn't back down. "How is he?"

"Mr. Thompson has suffered a myocardial infarction—what's commonly called a heart attack. It's caused by a sudden loss of blood to the heart, typically due to blockage of a coronary artery. The part of the heart muscle afflicted dies, and that causes chest pain and electrical instability, which in turn disrupts the heart's regular beat. Brain damage and death can result, but fortunately, Mr. Thompson was under the early care of paramedics. We'll have to monitor him for the next few days. We didn't have to do bypass surgery, but we'll want to perform additional tests to determine the extent of the damage and the prognosis. What kind of care will be available to him when he's released from the hospital?''

Ivy started to speak.

"He'll get the best," Linc intervened. He could afford it, and he'd make sure it happened. A gift whose source would remain unknown.

"He'll have to be in a cardiac rehabilitation program for several months. His activities for the next few weeks will have to be limited. He'll require help at home until he's fully ambulatory again. If help isn't available, he'll have to be in a nursing home, at least temporarily."

"He can move in with me," Ivy said, her voice barely above a whisper.

"Are you his granddaughter?"

"Yes," Ivy said with a stubborn tilt of her chin.

Linc shot her a look but chose not to argue right now. She couldn't possibly add taking care of Carl to her list of daily duties.

"Good," the doctor said. "He's being moved to CCU now. He won't wake up for some time yet, but you can see him for five minutes. Do you have any questions?"

Linc waited for Ivy to say something. When she didn't, he held out a hand, noting the physician's name and resolving to follow up later. "Thank you, Doctor."

"It's not unreasonable to expect him to make a full recovery with the proper care."

"He'll get it," Linc again promised. Beside him, Ivy only nodded and murmured her thanks, still caught in her trance.

The doctor left, and Linc turned Ivy in his arms, one finger beneath her chin tipping her face toward him.

She was so pale it worried him. "Ivy?" he prodded. "It's hopeful news, sweetheart."

Ivy lifted a ravaged gaze to his. "He's so hurt, Linc. He's too old to be enduring something like—" Her voice broke, and she ducked her head.

Linc enfolded her in his arms and held on. "Shh...sweetheart...he's going to make it. He's a tough old bird."

"I'm so afraid...I can't lose him." Her voice was a tortured whisper into his chest. "He's my family now. I can't lose anyone else."

Her sisters—that was what she must mean. "Do you want to look for them, Ivy? I'll help you, if you want."

"They're gone. Everyone is gone." She spoke in rote fashion.

Linc frowned and tried to lift her head to look into her eyes, but she only burrowed deeper into his chest. He abandoned his questions, relishing the feel of her in his arms. For this moment, he couldn't think about Betsey or his father, though their need for him was also great.

All he could feel, all he could think about, was Ivy, so defenseless. So alone.

The people of Palo Verde would do anything for her, he knew, but they depended on her to lead them. Depended on her strength. Right here, right now, Ivy's strength had fled.

She needed someone to be strong. He wanted it to be him.

"Come," he murmured into her hair, and led her back to the chairs. On impulse, he swept Ivy up in his arms and settled into one chair with her on his lap. Slowly and softly, he rocked her, tightening his arms around the fragile creature who moved him so, no matter how it complicated his life and upset his plans.

They sat there like that until the nurse came to lead them to Carl's bed.

As THEY WALKED down the hallway, Ivy held herself ramrod straight, though Linc could see the effort it required of her. He wished he could take her away and spare her, but the best he could do was walk close beside her and make sure she knew she was not alone. When they stood outside the CCU cubicle in which Carl had been placed, her small hand stole into his, and it felt like a victory.

He couldn't dwell on the bitter knowledge that Ivy trusted him, when he had lied to her from the start.

He shoved away those thoughts and gripped her hand. For a second, he thought he saw her shoulders relax a little in response.

Then the nurse stepped away, leaving no barrier between them and Carl.

Linc heard her gasp, felt her stiffen in shock and sway back a step before she dropped his hand and moved to Carl's side.

The old man was barely recognizable for all the tubes attached to him. The cubicle was a maze of beeping machines, whirring motors, inexplicable numbers on monitors. In that labyrinth lay the old man, his color almost as pale as the sheets on the bed.

Almost as pale as Ivy's face.

The setting was so foreign, so intimidating and sterile. So much like the room in which he'd last seen his father.

Guilt stabbed at Linc. He should be there with the man from whose seed he'd sprung. He should feel the same draw toward that man that he felt toward the one lying in this bed, a man he'd known for only days. He could picture Betsey at a bedside much like this, her lovely face pale and strained, too. Though he didn't understand her bond with the father who'd always been cold to him, he knew it was real. Knew Betsey was alone at that bedside.

And that she needed him.

But he had eyes only for Ivy. She reached for Carl's hand, careful to avoid the tubes and wires as she bent to place a kiss on his forehead. "I'm so sorry," she whispered.

Carl slept on, though.

"It was my fault," she said in a broken tone. "He didn't look well. He shouldn't have been in that position—"

Linc wrapped his fingers around Ivy's shoulders. He could feel her trembling against him. "I've read that unconscious people can sometimes hear what's said around them," he whispered in her ear. "If that's true, we have to be positive."

Ivy nodded faintly.

"You're going to be fine, Carl," Linc said. He touched Carl's shoulder, feeling the frail bones beneath his hand. "I'm taking Ivy home now, but we'll be back to see you." He refused to think about how long it might be before he could make that promise good.

The nurse stepped into the room. "Time's up."

Linc acknowledged her. Ivy didn't move.

"Ivy, we have to go now," he said gently.

Like an automaton, Ivy walked two steps with him, then tore out of his grasp and returned to Carl to hug him as best she could around all the tubes and wires. "I love you, Carl," she murmured.

When she came back, he could see the tears hovering at the tips of her lashes. She blinked them away, drawing into herself as he watched.

She needed to cry, but Linc didn't push just now. Instead, he escorted her out of the CCU and down the hallway toward the front door.

Ivy dug in her heels as they passed the waiting room. "I have to stay," she said.

He could hear the fear and exhaustion in her voice. "You heard the doctor. He'll sleep for hours yet. You won't be any good to him if you're worn-out yourself."

That chin jutted. "There's no one else."

"He has kids and grandkids, doesn't he?"

After a pause, Ivy nodded. "I don't know where they are, though."

"Someone will know. We'll ask Prudie or Lora Lee."

"Let's call them now. I'll wait here."

Linc looked at his watch. "Ivy, it's 1:00 a.m. We'll call them in the morning. You need some sleep."

The stubborn cast gave way to naked pain. "I can't leave him here alone."

"He's not alone. He's got plenty of people to watch over him. Come on, Ivy, you know I'm right." He softened his tone. "If you really want to help him, you'll be there when it counts the most. What will happen if you wear yourself down so much that you're useless when he gets home?"

He saw her resistance fade, but worry replaced it. "How am I going to take care of him when—" Her voice dwindled.

It wasn't hard to guess what she was thinking. Every hour of every day was already jammed full. She slept little enough as it was. He wanted to tell her that he'd be providing around-the-clock care for Carl at home—Carl's home, not Ivy's—as soon as he was released.

But an itinerant carpenter didn't have that kind of money.

And tonight was not the night for that discussion.

Instead, he drew her to him and pressed a kiss to her hair. "Tomorrow, Ivy. Tomorrow is soon enough to think about all that. Tonight you need to sleep."

Her eyes closed. "Maybe you're right," she said, her voice hollow.

"Come on," he said gently. "Let me take you home."

As though the last of her strength had ebbed,

she sagged against him. Linc swept her up in his arms and carried her out the front door.

HE THOUGHT she'd sleep on the way back, but she sat on her side of the truck, body stiff, hands clenched in her lap, and stared straight ahead. He tried a couple of conversational gambits, but she didn't respond. Finally, he gave up, his own thoughts in too much turmoil.

What should he do? He should already be back in Dallas, but he couldn't leave her tonight, not in this shape. She looked ready to shatter if the tension within her increased even a fraction.

And what about morning? What would he do then? She needed strength and support, reassurance and comfort. But the deeper he dug himself in, the more devastating it would be when she found out who he really was.

Linc tried to conjure some new solution to the problems of Palo Verde and his family's dilemma, but his own brain was beyond exhaustion. He'd had only an hour's sleep the night before this day of tumultuous emotions.

He should take his own advice. Let the night be, and figure out everything tomorrow.

As he pulled up before Ivy's cottage, he was relieved to see that no one waited for them. Maybe Aunt Prudie had called the hospital and found out

Carl was holding his own. At any rate, he was grateful. He couldn't handle any more emotional discussions tonight.

He rounded the hood of the truck and moved to the passenger side.

IVY FELT THE LOSS of Linc's presence even as she saw him coming around to her door. The door opened, and still she didn't move, unwilling to take the next step.

To be alone, as she'd been so often in her life.

She'd perfected her armor, girded herself with her smiles so no one would ever know the terror that lurked deep inside her, the terror that no one would ever truly want her, that she would always be, in the end, alone.

But tonight she couldn't seem to keep her armor in place. In its stead was a tissue-thin shield that buckled every time Linc reached out to comfort her.

Every time she thought of Carl and what he'd suffered because she hadn't been careful enough, hadn't been watchful enough over another person she loved.

Ivy knew Linc was waiting for her to alight so he could go. He'd made it clear earlier in the day that he had to leave. Only his kindness had kept him here this long.

She knew she should turn. Slip from the seat. Enter her house.

Let him go.

But she just couldn't. Not yet.

She heard the exasperated sigh. Felt his arms slide beneath her knees, around her back. He lifted her into his strong arms and headed toward her door. Soon he would enter, set her down, wish her goodbye—

And leave her life for good.

The thought of it sent steel-sharp agony into her heart.

He'd made no promises, she reminded herself. She'd asked for none. But tonight…oh, tonight, how she needed them. How she wished to pretend, if only for a few hours, that he was hers and she was his and there was nothing about her so wrong that he would, as had the others, abandon her. Like her father and her mother; like her sisters, who'd been torn away.

Her husband, who'd found her easy to leave.

Her baby, who'd slipped away.

As Linc set her down inside her house, she knew in a soul-deep and final way that she couldn't bear that tonight. So much did she dread the darkness of the night, the barrenness of her soul, that Ivy clung to him when he would have gone.

The last barrier cracked like dead tree limbs in winter. Tears dammed up too long burst free—

And Ivy wept.

"Ivy?" Linc's voice was both gentle and rough. "Oh, sweetheart—" He drew her to him, so close they shared one breath. Then he picked her up again and moved into her bedroom, where he settled into her rocking chair, cradling her on his lap.

She knew she was soaking the front of his shirt, and she tried to apologize, but he only shushed her and bundled her into the shelter of his strength.

Strong. He was so strong. So kind. He was the island of hope, of calm and peace in a world that had been so long turned on end.

Safe. Linc made her feel safe. She could barely remember the last time she'd had a guardian between her and a world determined to break her.

"Oh, Linc," she sobbed, reaching for his jaw, his cheek, the thick silk of his hair.

"Ivy, God, I—" Linc's voice died on a note of pain. His mouth descended on hers.

And the kiss was everything she'd longed for all her life. This was the kiss they'd begun but had feared to prolong. This was the kiss she'd waited for, the one she'd never thought to know.

Ivy kissed him back with all the hungers of her long-denied soul.

Her response electrified Linc, stripped away his

protective skin. Reached out to the boy who'd known nothing of comfort and love since the day his childhood died.

He couldn't get her close enough, couldn't drink in enough of her. All thought of any life beyond this moment vanished in the wake of Ivy's need. His need. Two souls too long denied.

He took the kiss deeper. Ivy moaned. Linc held her tightly in one arm, letting the other hand roam. He wanted to memorize her, to imprint himself on her. He wanted to touch the warmth that burned like a living coal inside her fragile shell. He'd felt Ivy's warmth, seen her love, and he wanted to claim both for himself. Wanted to make her his own.

He stood and strode to her bed. When he reached it, he waited until she opened her eyes.

It took a minute. Bliss stained her cheeks.

"Ivy…" he prodded softly. "Look at me."

Slowly, her lids lifted, her eyes glowing as he'd never seen them, but within them lay shadows.

He opened his mouth to speak, but she shook her head, her eyes pleading. Then, she slid slender fingers into his hair and brought his mouth to hers again.

For a second, Linc resisted. They should talk. He should tell her—

Ivy wouldn't wait.

So he gave in to a fight he had not the heart to make.

He lowered her to the bed in which he'd slept, his body aching for hers, and followed her down. Tonight was tonight. Tomorrow...

Would be here all too soon.

Ivy felt his resistance snap like a wire tightened too far, strained past its limits. There was such strength in him, such power. Such passion.

With exquisite care, he sent her flying, spun her beyond thought, past and future vanishing beneath the magic of his touch. He was the man she'd dreamed of all her life, and just when she'd accepted that dreams don't come true, here he was.

He was light in the darkness, hope chasing fear. Ivy's determination never to be vulnerable again fled in the face of this remarkable man, this wanderer who'd dropped into her life like a gift.

As his lips roamed her body, a pang grasped her heart. He was going to leave, and she had to stop him. She needed him. Palo Verde needed—

Then she thought no more, as Linc's hands trailed over her body, as his lips followed. As rapture sent her soaring.

Linc watched her fly and knew he'd met the only woman for him. Knew it the way he knew his own name. The way he knew his skin. She was part of him now, as essential as breath.

Then Ivy smiled, and his heart cracked. He had no words to explain to her what he'd done, no reasons that wouldn't hurt. Instead, he redoubled his efforts to make his body say what he could not yet voice.

He slid down her body, his own raging to mate, and forced himself to patience. He would make this night unforgettable for her and bind her to his heart. As he sought out secret valleys, as he heard her gasps and moans, he prayed for her forgiveness when the time came that she finally must know.

He tried to tell her the truths of the heart in the only way left to him now. As he suckled her breasts, as he tasted her tender secrets with his tongue, every caress, every kiss, was a wish. Every stroke a prayer.

Forgive me, Ivy. Please forgive.   Then it was Ivy pleading with him, dragging him upward, rocking her hips toward his. Her lips were red and puffy, her nipples tight, her eyes dark with longing. She was all he'd ever dreamed. More. The woman before him now was not sweet—

She was hungry. Her passion matched his own.

Mine, he wanted to shout. But didn't. Had no right.

So he locked his gaze on hers and lifted her hips in his big hands. "Look at me," he demanded.

She opened her eyes again, gripped his biceps with a strength that surprised him—

And smiled the smile of a woman with enough passion for a lifetime. Enough love for a world.

Rocked hard by yearning, he made them one.

He felt the shock race through her, echoing his own. The sense of belonging back to the beginning of time.

You're mine, Ivy Parker, whatever it takes. I can't let you go.

But even as he thought it, he knew he was wrong. He would have to leave and soon.

But he would be back. No matter what it took, he would not let this miracle go.

Then the magic between them caught fire, and Linc surrendered to the flames.

LINC AWOKE as the first pale strands of morning filtered in, feeling Ivy curled into him as though they'd always been one.

He thought of the night just passed, the ways they'd loved. Ivy's passion was as golden and beautiful as her love. She was the miracle he'd never dared believe in, the light he'd never known. To spend a lifetime with her, cherishing her, protecting her from harm and basking in her love…it was all his heart wanted. All he'd ever need.

All he could not have.

Not yet, his heart stubbornly insisted, the same heart that had carved a fortune from two hands, a life after banishment. Maybe not yet, but he refused to say never. It wouldn't be easy, but when hadn't his life been hard? Had that ever stopped him?

Hell, no. And it wouldn't stop him now.

Just then, Ivy stirred against him, and he knew he had to go. He couldn't explain now, not until he had a plan. But he had motivation aplenty to find a solution. Regardless of what he'd thought before, there was an answer here, an answer that would take care of both Ivy and the town she cared about.

But much as he wished it, that answer didn't lie in this bed. With regret, he rose and dressed, leaving her sleeping, this woman of his dreams.

Watching her from the doorway, memorizing every line of her frame, Linc was seized with a moment of terrible foreboding that if he left now, she would vanish and he would never find his way back to this heaven again.

But the businessman scoffed and the logical man sneered. All he had to do was use the brain that had been his salvation to find an answer to all that divided them now.

He needed a plan, and he was good at planning. He would find his answer.

Linc cast one last glance at Ivy's golden hair, spread over the pillow, at the soft rise of her breasts beneath the sheet, at the gentle smile curving her lips.

There was nothing he wanted more at this moment than to slide back in that cocoon with her, to lock out the world for just one more day.

But that was what the heart wanted—

And the heart couldn't always have the last say.

CHAPTER TEN

IVY AWOKE BY INCHES, wrapped in the soft shawl of pleasure so voluptuous she wanted to linger inside it.

She turned over, snuggling into her pillow, inhaling a scent that curved her lips, the scent of—

Her eyes flew open.

Linc.

She bolted up on the bed, memories skittering: his powerful body poised over hers, his eyes by turns soft and blazing hot, his hands, his lips....

The pillow beside her bore the imprint of his head, but the covers had been pulled up, hiding any other sign that he'd been here.

"Linc?" she inquired quietly. Was she ready to face him after she'd lost her mind in his arms?

Then other images poured over her: Linc sitting beside her in the waiting room, restless but determined to stay; Linc with the doctor—

Carl. She leaped from the bed, seeking her robe—

She froze. Naked. She'd never slept naked in her

life, but she'd been naked with Linc, in more than one way.

From the closet she grabbed her gown and robe, slipped the gown over her head, cinched the robe around her. Feeling a little more armed to face him, she ventured from the room in search of first Linc, then her phone.

Nothing. Not a sign, not a note. Was he sorry for what he'd done?

A horrified thought struck her. Had it been out of pity?

Then a more awful thought hit: what if something had happened to Carl? With shaking fingers, she found the hospital number and dialed the phone.

After a series of transfers, she sagged against her kitchen wall. Carl was weak, but he was awake, already crabbing to the nurses, giving them grief.

Ivy smiled. He would be all right. She would make sure of it, no matter what was required.

Then she remembered the doctor's stern warnings. Recalled Linc's assurances that Carl would get whatever he needed.

Where are you, Linc? And how can you promise things that cost the earth?

Or did he plan to stay and help her?

Ivy couldn't decide how to feel. A part of her heart lifted at the possibility he wouldn't leave after all. Another part shrank from facing him after last night. She'd lost herself so completely. She'd never known lovemaking could be like that. Jimmy had never made her feel so transported, so—

Hot. Even through her embarrassment, Ivy had to smile. She'd been like gunpowder lit by a match. She'd become someone she didn't know, a woman lifted from despair to boneless delight, a creature of the body, a being who hungered.

It was more than physical, though...and that was too scary by half. Linc had stroked her body, but he'd also reached down inside and touched her soul. She'd felt a bond with him that made her shiver still. Yet she knew so little about him. And that was where the problem lay. Even if she'd been ready to involve herself with a man again, how could she possibly trust herself to someone so closed in, so enigmatic? He was a wanderer, a loner. When her judgment of Jimmy had been so flawed though she'd known him well, how could she so blithely leap into the arms of a virtual stranger?

She and Linc had to talk. She couldn't afford to give him the wrong impression—at least, not any more than she'd already done, she corrected. Oh God. How could she have fallen so far, so fast?

But she had to find him first.

Glancing at the clock, Ivy gasped. The café should have been opened an hour ago.

She raced from her kitchen, brushed her teeth and threw on some clothes, then ran across the grass.

No, she chided herself. Linc would have to wait. As soon as there was a break, she had to go visit Carl before anything else.

Not that she was a coward, she told herself. Just that other things needed to come first.

LINC HANDED his father's gardener, Aaron, the keys to his truck and retrieved his Jaguar keys with thanks. "Sorry I had to keep the truck for longer than I thought. I'll take care of the bill for the one you had to rent for work."

"No problem," replied Aaron, casting a longing glance at the Jag. "That beauty really impressed my grandson when he came to visit."

Linc grinned, grateful for the relief from his dark thoughts. Leaving Ivy was a thorn under his skin. He itched to go back, but a call to Betsey en route had made it clear he was running out of time.

A half hour later, he entered his hotel suite, his mind on the thousand and one things he had to accomplish this day. He strode to the desk, opened his laptop and booted up. While he waited to check his e-mail, he would take a shower. Crossing the room, he stripped off his shirt—

And caught the scent of flowers and cinnamon. Of Ivy.

He stopped in his tracks and gripped the shirt, leaning against the closet door as yearning punched him in the gut. At this moment, there was nothing he craved more than to go back, to see her. To hold her once more.

Would she find his note? There'd been so little he could say. Would it be enough?

He already feared it would not. Thoughts of Ivy waking up without him had haunted him every mile of the trip. She had such a tender heart, such an open, unprotected soul. Even if she wasn't vulnerable because of the load she carried or her inevitable worries over Carl, she was heart without borders, a spirit that could be crushed.

No, he amended. Ivy was stronger than that. She wouldn't be crushed.

But she would be hurt. She wouldn't understand, could have no idea how he felt, how he'd treasured last night, how he'd never forget her and wished to God he could.

Linc shook his head violently and straightened, clamping down on thoughts that were tearing him apart. It was too late—the damage was done. By leaving Ivy so abruptly, he had hurt someone who would not herself hurt a soul. He would have to live with that.

But he wouldn't stop trying to find a way to make it up to her.

Right now, though, that had to wait. Betsey needed him, and his father lay in a bed dying. He couldn't torture himself any more with thoughts of Ivy or Carl or all he wished he could do for them to change the fate of the small town they loved.

Or all he wanted to do for a woman who, in a space of days, had opened a place inside him he'd thought long dead.

Shoving away from the door frame, Linc tossed aside the shirt and its haunting, seductive scent.

And stepped into the shower to begin to wash Palo Verde away.

IVY CLIMBED THE STAIRS, wondering what she'd find. She already knew Linc's truck was gone. She'd wanted to ask Mabel if he'd said anything to her before he left, but even if Ivy had known how to ask without her voice or face betraying her, they'd been too busy to talk. Mabel had gotten the café open, started coffee and been cooking for the first customers when Ivy arrived, out of breath from running. Mabel had barely paused to pass along the next orders before moving out to take up her normal routine, her lifted eyebrows and searching glance the only sign that something was different.

Ivy wished she could avoid the inevitable discussion, but the best she'd been able to do was to tell Mabel she'd be right back and slip up the stairs before Mabel could ask where she was going.

Her heart gave a little hitch as she neared Linc's bedroom. The door stood open, but she paused before going inside.

There had been mornings when he'd left in his truck, but he'd always returned for breakfast. For all she knew, he could be visiting Carl or already at work on one of the buildings on the square.

But deep inside, she already knew he was not.

Squaring her shoulders, she stepped into the room.

Empty. Empty of more than his meager belongings. Somehow the room itself seemed forlorn. Barren.

But she could catch his scent of clean, healthy male. A thin ribbon of it curled in the room, a reminder of a man who had no need for artifice.

Tears rushed to her eyes, and she remembered crying her heart out in his arms last night. *Oh, Linc…why? What did I do?*

Then she saw the scrap of paper lying on the bureau top. Her fingers clenched, then released as she stood frozen, almost superstitious about what it might be. If it was the note she hadn't found in her cottage, it meant he was truly gone. If she didn't read it, she could still hope.

What nonsense, Ivy Parker. He never promised to stay. She forced her head high. With determined steps, she crossed the room.

Ivy, said the bold scrawl on the outside. She realized she'd never seen his handwriting. Like the man, it was strong and sure.

With fingers that weren't quite steady, she picked the note up.

I have to leave, Ivy. I'm sorry. I wish I could stay.

Linc

With a small cry, she crushed the paper in her fist, last night's dreams torn from her heart.

"Ivy, honey?" Aunt Prudie's voice sounded from the doorway.

Startled, Ivy kept her back turned until she could shove away the heartache that crowded her throat. "Good morning, Aunt Prudie," she said, her voice wavering.

"What's wrong? Where are Linc's things?"

Ivy pinched her nose and blinked back tears of weakness. "He—he left."

"Left? After what happened yesterday? How can he leave when you need him here?"

"He, uh—" Ivy sniffed again, then found her voice. "He had some things to take care of. He told me yesterday before everything happened that he had to go."

"Carl—how is he?" Aunt Prudie asked, her own voice quavering a bit. "I called the hospital, but they wouldn't tell me anything specific."

Ivy straightened and faced her. "He's in intensive care. He suffered a heart attack, but he's stable now. They're running a lot of tests to see what the damage is and how long he'll have to stay. They're concerned about his age." She found a tiny smile. "But he's already giving the nurses grief, so that's a good sign."

For once, Prudie didn't have an acerbic remark ready. "Linc went after you. Didn't he find you?"

Ivy's eyes flooded again. Desperately, she looked away, out the window. "Yes," she whispered. "He stayed with me until Carl was stable and then he brought me home—" Her voice cracked.

"Oh, honey, I'm so sorry. I had such hopes for the two of you." Prudie crossed the floor and took Ivy in her arms, holding her against her slight frame. "What happened? Why did he go?"

Ivy sagged against her great-aunt, clasping

Linc's crumpled note in one hand. "I don't know," she whispered. "I just don't know. What makes me so easy to leave, Aunt Prudie?"

"Oh, sweetheart, it isn't you," Prudie soothed. Her voice hardened. "I thought he was made of more than that, but you're better off without him if that's not the case. He doesn't deserve you."

Her great-aunt's consoling words did nothing to ease the ache in Ivy's heart. Last night had been so—

She tightened her jaw and forced herself away from the frail old woman's shoulder. Last night had been an illusion, that was all. Ivy reached into her apron pocket but found no tissue to use.

Prudie seemed to understand what she needed and drew one from the pocket of her robe. "It's all right to cry, Ivy honey."

Ivy took the proffered tissue and shook her head. "No," she said in a voice strangled by tears. "Tears do no one any good." She'd cried in Linc's arms and look what had come of it. She drew in a long, hitching breath. "I'm going to see Carl after I close. Would you like to come?"

Prudie looked as though she wanted to say something that Ivy was sure she didn't want to hear. Seeming to think better of it, Prudie merely nodded before answering. "Of course I do. Someone needs to stop that old goat from terrorizing the nurses.''

Ivy smiled a little, then drew in another deep breath, feeling her insides settle a bit. "And who better than you to take him on? I'd better go downstairs. I've got a café to run.''

Aunt Prudie hesitated and grasped Ivy's hand before she could leave. "Just you remember that the fault is in him, Ivy girl, not in you.''

Ivy knew her great-aunt wasn't speaking about Carl. With a squeeze of the woman's tiny hand, Ivy nodded. "Thank you, Aunt Prudie.'' Ivy hugged her for a long time, then left the room.

IVY PAUSED AT THE DOORWAY to Carl's hospital room, realizing Aunt Prudie wasn't beside her. Glancing over her shoulder, she saw that the older woman had stopped in the hall and was staring straight ahead, toward his bed, her expression troubled.

"Aunt Prudie?'' she asked. "Are you all right?''

With a shock, she realized Prudie's eyes brimmed with tears.

When the older woman caught Ivy's worried gaze, she pulled herself upright, almost military rigid. "Well, don't just stand there gawking. No telling what havoc the man is wreaking on these poor nurses.'' She brought one of the tissues she always had stuck in a pocket or sleeve to her nose.

Ivy hesitated, wondering what to say.

"Hon, you're gonna catch flies if you don't close that mouth.'' Aunt Prudie's expression defied pity.

Ivy went on instinct and gave her aunt a quick grin. "Let's go—we wouldn't want any more wear and tear on the nurses, would we?'' She bustled into the room.

"Hi, Carl. How are you feeling?'' Ivy tried to ignore all the equipment beeping and humming around him. Instead, she closed the distance to the bed and leaned over to kiss his cheek. "You look great.''

"Good grief.'' Aunt Prudie sidled around her. "You'll give the old goat a swelled head.''

"Humph. Who invited you, old woman?'' But Carl's usual bluster had little force.

Ivy saw Prudie's eyes shimmer and her hands tighten on the crumpled tissue.

She intervened. "We're both so glad to see you.'' She squeezed his fingers, careful to avoid the IV needle taped to the back of his gnarled hand. "You can be as cranky as you want.'' She pasted on a determined smile. "Are you hungry? I brought you some pie.''

His eyes drifted down. "Not just now, Ivy.'' He

forced them open. "How are you, little girl? How is Stevie?"

"I'm—" Her throat jammed. She cleared it. "Stevie's doing fine. Thanks to you. You saved her." Suddenly, her vision blurred. "Oh, Carl, I'm so sorry. This is all my fault."

"Don't you try to take the blame for this, young lady," he scolded. "You take too much on those shoulders of yours. Why, you're little bigger than a minute, and you shouldn't—"

An alarm shrilled. Ivy frantically searched the monitors to figure out what was wrong. The nurse rushed in. "Step back, please. She pressed a spot on one screen, frowning. Then she pressed another one and felt Carl's pulse, staring at the clock over his bed. Finally, she nodded. "Mr. Thompson, your guests will have to leave now."

"But—" Ivy protested. "I haven't—"

The nurse's look was gentle but firm. "Mr. Thompson must rest now. He can't be upset."

"I didn't mean to—"

The nurse drew Ivy aside and placed one hand on Ivy's arm. "Many people become upset when they see a loved one in such a foreign environment. I know the equipment can be intimidating, and it's not easy to feel comfortable here." She gave Ivy's arm a pat. "Mr. Thompson is receiving the best of care. I promise you that we're watching over him.

Mr. Thompson's heart doesn't need additional stress. Rest is the best thing for him, but he does need to know his loved ones are near. If you can control yourself and not yield to emotion, I'll give you another minute or two to speak with him and say goodbye for now.''

The woman's no-nonsense attitude steadied Ivy. ''I'll be careful,'' Ivy promised.

The nurse smiled and gave her one more pat. ''That's good.'' Then she left.

Aunt Prudie hung back, but Ivy neared Carl's bed, noticing the tracery of blue veins beneath his skin, the lines the years had carved into his features. He looked so frail. He wasn't the Carl she'd come to count on. Tenderness slid past her fear, and she felt her strength returning, displacing the bitter tang of guilt.

Carl needed her to be strong. She would be strong.

''You're going to be fine, Carl,'' she said. ''The doctor told Linc and me last night that you can make a full recovery. You're just going to have to be patient.''

''I'm ready to go home,'' he muttered. ''Don't like hospitals. People die in hospitals.''

''Well, you're not going to die, Carl Thompson.'' Prudie's voice was a little shaky but gathered strength. ''You're too ornery. Good Lord is still hoping you'll come to your senses. He's got work to do on you yet."

Carl's lack of response was more worrisome than all the machines. His eyelids drooped.

"We'd better go now," Ivy said. She leaned over to kiss him goodbye.

"My family know yet?" he asked.

"Lora Lee called them. She had to leave a message for your son, but your daughter and her family are on their way. They should be here this afternoon."

"You'll let them in my house, Ivy girl?" he said weakly. "Get them settled? Linc can help you out."

Stunning and quick, the pain sliced deep. But Linc wasn't his problem. Carl shouldn't be worrying about anyone but himself. She was about to answer when Aunt Prudie spoke.

"Boy's gone, Carl. Left Ivy high and dry."

Carl's eyes flew open. "How could he do that?" Just then an alarm went off again.

"Shh, Carl," Ivy said, shoving away the pain of Linc's abandonment. "He always said he had to leave, and I don't need him." The lie stuck in her throat, but she swallowed it. She could hear the nurse bustling in behind her.

"I'm afraid you must leave now."

Ivy felt sick. "We're leaving." She leaned over

Carl. "Don't you worry about a thing. We're all doing fine, and we'll make sure your family is cared for." She leaned over the railing, past all the tubes and wires, and brought her cheek against his, cradling the other cheek in her hand. "I love you, Carl. We all do. You just rest."

The nurse moved up beside her.

Ivy drew away but kept her gaze on Carl's. "You're going to be just fine." She stepped back to make way for Aunt Prudie.

"Place isn't the same without you, Carl Thompson," Aunt Prudie said in a gruff voice. "You quit malingering and get yourself back to Palo Verde."

"Always bossin' me around, aren't you, Prudie?" But a faint smile teased his lips as his eyes drifted shut.

Ivy clasped Aunt Prudie's hand, then touched the nurse on the arm. "I'm really sorry. I wouldn't hurt him for the world."

The woman's eyes softened. "I believe that. It's hard to see the ones you love brought low." Then she smiled. "I promise you he's in good hands."

"We can come back?" Ivy asked. She didn't know what she'd do if they wouldn't let her see him.

The nurse studied her for a minute, then nodded. "If you can keep things light and easy on him."

Ivy wrapped her arm around Aunt Prudie's

shoulders, surprised to feel a faint tremble in her frame. "We'll do better, won't we, Aunt Prudie?"

Aunt Prudie straightened. "You bet your boots we will."

The nurse smiled. "We'll see you later, then."

Arm in arm, Ivy and her great-aunt walked slowly back to Ivy's car.

LINC STOOD OUTSIDE the mansion that should have felt like home. Suddenly, the door opened and there she was.

"Linc! Oh, Linc—" Betsey threw herself into his arms and hugged him fiercely.

After a second's hesitation, he returned the hug, unable to wipe from his mind the last time a woman had wept in his embrace. Model-thin, clad in a sleek designer dress that showed off her long legs, Betsey was taller than Ivy, her body more angular and bony than Ivy's, with its sweet womanly curves. Her scent of subtly enticing, very expensive perfume wafted to his nose.

He fought a heartfelt wish for flowers and cinnamon.

Finally, the flow of tears ceased. Betsey looked up at him from beneath thick lashes, green eyes as lovely as ever. For a traitorous instant, he compared her still-perfect makeup and expertly coiffed hair with Ivy's flour-smudged cheeks, unpainted mouth, untamed hair.

And found Betsey wanting.

"What is it?" she asked, vulnerable and searching.

Reminding himself of all she'd been through and how much she needed him, he shoved away thoughts of Ivy. "Nothing."

"You look tired. Come in here and let me get you a drink." Betsey clasped his hand and drew him with her to the library, which had been his father's retreat from the noise of two boys. The room smelled, as it always had, of expensive leather bindings overlaid with the faint notes of pipe tobacco. "How is…Carl, is it?"

"He's going to be fine." Linc hoped it was true. He'd already arranged for nursing care and would receive regular reports. Still, he wished he could have stayed to talk to the old man.

"Linc, who's Ivy?"

His head snapped up. "She's just…someone I met in Palo Verde. One of the tenants."

One eyebrow arched. "Linc, are you sure you're all right?"

"Of course." Guilt sharpened his voice. With effort, he softened it. He couldn't discuss Ivy with her. "I'm fine, Bets. Tell me how you are."

Lifting a bottle of his favorite well-aged Scotch

from the gleaming mahogany sideboard near his father's massive desk, she hesitated.

He wished he'd asked for coffee. He had a quick vision of thick, welcoming mugs served by a gentle, hardworking hand. Ruthlessly, he banished it, seeing Betsey's hand shake. She set the bottle down. "He's refusing his pain medication until he can speak with you."

"I'd better go see him, then. Forget the Scotch." With something akin to relief, he headed for the door.

"Linc, wait—"

He paused, then faced her. Normally a woman of immense inner poise, Betsey twisted her slender manicured fingers, then stopped and gripped them.

"What is it?" he asked.

"If he—" She didn't meet his gaze. "There are things he wants from you, but you—" Her voice descended to little more than whisper. She lifted her eyes to his. "Don't do anything you don't want, Linc. Promise me that. I don't want that from you."

He frowned. "What do you mean?"

Her gaze slid away. She shook her head. "I shouldn't have said that much." Green eyes locked on his. "Go see him, Linc. He really regrets what happened between you." Betsey paused. "I do, too."

"Betsey, what is this about?" A chill invaded his bones.

She only shook her head and moved past him to open the door. "Come, I'll walk with you."

Linc wanted to detain her, to make her explain herself, but just then he noticed her fingers gripping the door handle. Saw evidence of her nerves and realized just how much his father's dying was extracting from her. For whatever reason, his father meant a great deal to Betsey, and the fondness was returned. His father had never been a sentimental man, but in their few conversations since he'd been summoned back, Linc had recognized the bond between them.

It shouldn't have surprised him. She had, after all, chosen his family over him a long time ago.

WHEN AUNT PRUDIE WENT upstairs to take her nap, Ivy made her pies for the next day as usual, trying to find respite from her thoughts in rolling out flaky crusts and mixing the fillings. For the first time in her memory, cooking did not soothe her.

It was too quiet. The café lay around her, empty of life. Carl wasn't sitting in his usual chair, complaining about what was wrong with the world or telling her about what he'd seen on the goldarn foolish television last night. Stevie wasn't playing in the corner, needing attention. She couldn't see

Linc across the square, on the roof of one of the nearby buildings—

Ivy bowed her head, stilled her fingers on the rolling pin—

The neat circle of crust blurred.

He was gone. Dull dread had replaced the shock of the morning's discovery. She'd soared to heights of bliss last night that she'd never imagined. Even more enticing had been the safety of his strong arms, the freedom to cry at last, to be the comforted.

She'd thought she'd found her safe place, her harbor. Found the home of her heart.

But it had all been a dream, vanished in morning's merciless light.

For the first time since her baby's life had slipped from her body and a barren emptiness had taken over, Ivy had felt, last night, an easing of a sorrow too deep for tears. Despite her worries for Carl and her guilt over what had befallen him, she had known a healing of the endless grief and loss around which she'd built a protective shell.

She'd opened herself last night and let Linc inside.

Finding him gone without a word this morning had left her bleeding, her shell shattered.

For a moment, Ivy wanted to sink to the floor, curled in a ball. Wanted to howl out her pain and rage. She'd let herself believe last night had meant something. That he might stay after all.

Ivy clutched at the rolling pin and pressed down so hard she split the crust.

No. Down that road lay madness, lay more of the desolation of the past year. She would not give it power. She'd worked too hard to rise again from the darkness.

With unsteady fingers, she pieced the crust and carefully positioned it in the pie pan, determined to salvage it as she would salvage the rest of her life from last night's misstep.

That was all it was, all she could let it be.

A simple mistake. A misunderstanding between two strangers.

Ruthlessly, Ivy buried memories of Linc's strong arms, of his hot, dangerous, haunted eyes…of the glory she'd felt before this morning's crash to earth.

I wish I could stay, his note had said. No promises to cling to, no hope created. She'd never know what the sadness in his eyes meant, but at least he hadn't left her waiting for a return that would never come.

It was an honesty she'd consider a mercy, she was sure. Maybe not today when her heart was so sore, but…

Someday.

Enough of that. She dusted off her hands. As soon as she was finished with the pies, she'd go to Sally's and check on the baby. Then she had wallpaper to hang. If it took the rest of a night when she knew sleep would be elusive, all to the good.

CHAPTER ELEVEN

LINC'S STEPS SLOWED as he ascended the sweeping mahogany stairway and followed Betsey toward the master suite of a house that was a tomb, a lifeless monument to money. Once, it had been a warm place where his mother had played hide-and-seek and read stories, but after her death, it had settled into cold, sterile spaces barely touched by his father and the silent, efficient drones who served him. Linc and Garner had been brushed away into the corners of his father's life.

For an agonizing second, Linc thought about Ivy's homey cottage, about the café she'd turned into the town's center. Both were shabby, both in dire need of repair—but both exploded with life, vibrant and rich. Children played...people shared a fellowship created by one small woman, determined to save the world.

God, he missed her. Missed them all.

For the first time in hours, he allowed himself to think about the note that he knew now was all wrong. Fresh from Ivy's bed and her voluptuous yet oddly innocent body, he hadn't been able to find words to explain his complicated situation. Honor wouldn't let him make promises he couldn't keep, but that hadn't kept him from wanting to make them. Despite all the reasons he knew he couldn't, he wanted to be back in Palo Verde more than he'd ever wanted to be anywhere since his mother died. He wanted to argue with Carl. Wanted to listen to Prudie and Mabel gossip. Wanted to try playing with Stevie, mystery though the baby was.

"Linc?" Betsey broke into his thoughts, and he realized he'd come to a halt outside the doorway of his father's room.

"What?"

She reached for his hand and squeezed. "I should prepare you. He's much worse than when you saw him last."

A week ago, just barely. But a lifetime.

Linc shoved thoughts of Palo Verde into the far recesses of his mind and nodded. "I'm ready."

Her eyes swam with sympathy as she opened the door.

A few steps behind her on the thick champagne carpet, Linc was glad for the distance that allowed him to compose himself.

Old. His father was truly old. And dying. Death rode his features almost as hard as pain.

His eyes, locked on Linc, were Linc's own. His bold nose, his harsh, once unyielding jaw were still there, though stripped of their power, softened as jagged cliffs are blunted by rain and wind.

Linc paused, staring away from the huge poster bed to the too-dark paneling, the lifeless designer perfection. In the mirror on the far wall, Linc saw with shock how much he resembled his father as he'd been, the man he'd once wanted so badly to be proud of him, to love him...to approve. The man he'd fought to free himself from for fifteen years.

He didn't like it. Didn't want to think he might have become the same man.

"Lincoln." His father's voice, once so strong, was a bare whisper now. "Come here."

Not *please*. Not *will you*. For a second, the young, angry Linc wanted to refuse, to walk away, to shift the balance.

Betsey's glance at him pleaded. Linc looked at the husk of the man he'd once feared and knew a moment's intense pity that would wound his father worse than any rebellion ever had.

Pity mingled with embarrassment and dread. Dread of ever being this helpless, of ever being this unloved. Of being a man with two sons who'd cared for neither. Who'd banished one and made the other feel so inadequate that he'd forfeited his life.

At that moment Linc understood something his father had never known, and his heart relented. He was different after all. He'd learned from Ivy that everyone was valuable, anyone worthy of caring. His father had never understood that. *He* was the man locked in poverty, more so than those people living on a shoestring in Palo Verde.

Sadness for his father's loss propelled him forward. "Father," he said, trying with only partial success to keep emotion from his voice. "How are you feeling?"

Anger rose past the weariness for a second. "How do you think I—?" Anger sputtered. Died. His father exhaled heavily. "Son, I—" He glanced away, his jaw working.

Son. How long Linc had waited to hear that. He'd been no man's son for fifteen years. Fury at the waste of years, at the love allowed to wither, stung his heart. Garner would still be alive if not for this man's insistence on perfection, his blindness to his youngest son's troubled soul.

But Linc had been blind, too. Hadn't even bothered to look. If he'd ever checked, would he have seen the pressure grinding his brother past bearing?

"Your brother left an unfortunate situation—"

Linc exploded. "Don't you blame him. You

could have helped him. Why didn't you see what you were doing to him? All he ever wanted was your approval, your love—''

"Linc—'' Betsey pleaded.

He whirled on her. "No, don't put yourself in the middle again, Betsey. This is between us.'' He turned back to his father. "But you couldn't love either of us, could you? You don't have the faintest idea what goes on in the heart—''

"I loved you.''

"You did not.'' Linc stared at him. "You hated me.''

"I was proud of you,'' his father said.

"You're lying.''

His father continued as if Linc hadn't spoken. "Too proud. I saw myself in you. I knew you would one day surpass my accomplishments, that you had the mind and the courage and the heart to accomplish anything you wanted.''

Linc jerked his gaze away, bitterness crawling up his throat and choking him. If it was true, why had he never said so to Linc? Not one time had his father breathed a word of it to a boy starved for the slightest crumb of approval.

"I placed all my hopes on your young shoulders, and when you headed down your own path, I tried to discipline the rebellion out of you, but it didn't work. We only grew farther and farther apart.'' His look asked Linc for understanding Linc couldn't give. "I was middle-aged when you were born. Your mother and I were not a love match, though love grew between us. I married her to have sons, to pass on the empire I was building. But your mother was the link between us, the one who understood love and playing in the grass and appreciating a ray of sunshine through a window."

A spasm of pain washed over his features, and his breath caught.

"Edward, let me give you your medication now." Betsey rushed to his other side, reaching for a bottle.

"No," he snapped. Then he reached out his hand. "I'm sorry, Betsey. I can't have my head fuzzy right now." Betsey gripped his hand. On her face, Linc could see honest affection and more than a little fear. Not fear *of* his father, though. Fear *for* him.

Linc spoke through a clenched jaw. "You sent me away. You told me never to come back."

"What was I supposed to do? Let you keep rebelling until you destroyed all of us? Did you ever stop to think what you were doing to Betsey with that stunt? What about your brother?"

There it was, the poison arrow. For the rest of his life, Linc would carry with him the memory of his last glimpse of his brother's face, naked with pain and hatred as Linc returned after spending the night with the woman Garner had loved and planned to marry.

Guilt wrapped Linc in its thorny tendrils, imprisoning him in the sunless world of this house. Even if he could explain that angry young man, it was too late to help Garner. Forever too late.

The waste of it sickened him. ''You had your perfect son. What happened?''

''If your mother—'' His father's voice failed. He closed his eyes for a moment, seeming to struggle for the strength to finish.

Betsey held out a glass of water, placing the straw against his lips.

''Don't talk,'' Linc said.

His father finished sipping and lay back, exhausted and paler than ever. Still, his eyes crackled. ''I'll have my say.''

For a moment, the old animosity shimmered between them, two powerful males, each bent on domination.

His father looked away first. ''When your mother died, she left a hole bigger than I knew how to fill. I had no idea how to comfort two small boys who cried in the night. All I knew how to do was to make money, and if it hadn't been enough to save Amelia, I'd make sure it was enough to protect the two of you. So I concentrated on doing what my father had always done, and his father, and his father before him. I worked. I made money for my family and let other people comfort my sons." His voice grew ragged. "I told myself that you were better off, and as each year went by, it became easier to believe that. I did well at the only thing I knew how to do. When you kept getting into trouble, I took it as a direct rebuke of everything I was doing and focused on driving out your rebellious streak.

"And in so doing, I lost the son who'd always been my shining hope." He stared straight ahead, not at Linc, and spoke again. "Garner knew it, somehow, though I never said a word. He wasn't as strong as you, Linc." The eagle eyes pierced him again. "He cared too much."

Linc was still reeling from his father's declarations. His father's shining hope? If the sun had come up in the west, it couldn't have unsettled him more. Already weary from the emotion of last night and of this morning's parting, Linc couldn't, for the life of him, figure out what he felt.

So he swept his confusion into a dark corner and simply asked, "You knew where I was, didn't you? The entire time."

His father nodded.

"Why didn't you tell Garner? I could have helped him."

"Would you have?" his father challenged. "You knew where he was. You could have checked on him."

Linc was only too aware of that. To his dying day, he would live with the power of his regret.

"You can do something for him now," his father said.

Linc's head came up. "What?"

"You can make it up to Garner, all of it, by protecting what he cared about most."

Linc's eyes narrowed. "What was that?"

His father's gaze locked on his. "Betsey. Marry her. Take care of her for him."

"Edward, no—" Betsey gasped. "I asked you not to."

"You loved Linc once. Garner wasn't your first choice. Don't think I didn't understand that."

"Oh, please, tell me Garner didn't know." Her eyes filled with tears, darting between his father and Linc. "I cared about Garner, and I came to love him—"

"But not the way you loved Linc," his father said. "And he loved you." His gaze swiveled to Linc's. "Didn't you?"

Turmoil rendered Linc speechless. Yes, he'd loved Betsey, but—

Now there was Ivy. He closed his eyes for a

second, searching for the warmth Ivy had brought into his life, but all he could feel was dread and cold.

"Linc? Remember what I said." Her voice wavered. "You don't have to."

Linc stared at Betsey, trying to find the girl he'd loved so fiercely inside the stranger standing across his father's deathbed. What did he know of the woman she'd become?

Yet how could he desert her when her world had crumbled? She'd always had anything her heart desired. She had never had a job, never learned how to manage the harsh realities of life. Garner had kept her in a bubble, and his father had continued the practice. Now she was stone-cold broke. And selling a dozen dusty, worn-out buildings in Palo Verde wouldn't ever return her to her former life.

Despite all that, Betsey hadn't turned mean, hadn't struck out to blame anyone. If she didn't have Ivy's heart or Ivy's courage, she had virtues of her own. She was loyal to a fault—hadn't their aborted romance proved that? She could have deserted his father after Garner's death and sought out the attentions of other wealthy men—heaven knows she was beautiful enough to be snapped up right away.

But she hadn't. She'd stayed by the side of a dying man, a man who was now asking Linc to do right by her, to safeguard a woman who'd never learned to take care of herself.

A woman he'd once thought he loved beyond bearing.

"Lincoln, I can't be there for her any longer…" His father's hard-fought breath rasped on Linc's hearing.

"No, Linc," Betsey said dully. "It's not necessary. You've done enough."

No. He hadn't, not for anyone. Not for Garner. Not for Betsey. Not for—

Ivy. What would Ivy do in his place?

He knew already. She'd never once thought of herself when others were in need.

Inside, Linc rebelled. He wanted more time— time to explain to Ivy, time to make things right, time to cherish her and warm himself at her fire, time to win her love.

At the thought of Ivy's love, Linc's heart tore. He'd forfeited that when he'd lied, then walked away after a night beyond a man's dreams.

He bowed his head, staring at his shoes. What right did he have to go after his heart's desire when his brother had paid for Linc's mistakes with his life? The long road to Garner's death had begun with Linc's rebellion. Agreeing to this would not make up for what he'd done, but it would be a start. One day, perhaps he could look at himself in the mirror again without loathing.

But he had to make things better for Ivy, somehow. And soon, though not in the way he wanted. His path lay elsewhere.

The hell of it was, Ivy would understand better than anyone.

He lifted his head to look at Betsey for several moments, then shifted his gaze to his father's. Breathing from a chest tight with all he would never have, he answered his father. "All right. I'll marry Betsey. I'll take care of her."

His father's eyes closed in relief. Linc heard Betsey's soft sob and looked at her.

Green eyes swimming with tears, slender fingers over her mouth, Betsey was a study in confusion—worry laid over hope, relief vying with embarrassment. "Linc..."

Linc summoned a smile he hoped someday he could really feel. "It'll be all right, Bets, I promise." Silently, he said goodbye to Ivy in his heart.

Unable to stand any more emotion, he took his leave of his father and walked out of the room to pick up the pieces of a life that had changed beyond recognition.

IVY CLOSED THE DOOR behind the last customer, barely resisting the urge to lean against it. She felt as though she could sleep around the clock, but there were pies to bake for tomorrow and floors to mop. She wanted to see Carl again during visiting hours tonight. She'd bake his favorite apple again, just in case he'd be allowed to eat it, and take some cookies to the nursing staff.

"Hon, you sit down over there and let me clean up this time," Mabel offered.

Ivy faced her. "Thanks, but you've got that grandbaby coming over tonight, don't you?"

Mabel beamed. "The only good thing that came out of that good-for-nothing my daughter married. But I can spare an hour. You sit down, now."

Ivy shook her head. "It's time to bake the pies. How about if I make an extra one for you? Howard just brought me some lovely peaches. What about peach pie?"

"You've got extra pies in the freezer, hon. Just this once, cut yourself some slack and use them for tomorrow. You're dead on your feet."

Ivy found a missed crumb on one table and scooped it up, avoiding the older woman's eyes. "A little later, maybe." If she closed her eyes, she'd only see Linc.

Mabel's arm stole around her, the reassuring bulk of her spreading warmth into the empty cold that had been Ivy's heart. For a split second, she sagged against Mabel's ample side.

"You poor thing." Mabel's voice went as tight and fierce as her hug. "I could kill that man."

Ivy wanted the comfort, but blaming Linc wasn't fair. "He never said he'd stay, Mabel."

"Doesn't matter," Mabel muttered. "You deserve a family, same as anyone else. More, even."

Ivy smiled and almost felt it. "I have you and Aunt Prudie and Carl and all the others."

"Not the same, and you know it." Mabel shook her head. "Still, we've got the better part of the bargain."

This smile was not so forced. "No, you don't," Ivy said. Linc might be gone, and with him her half-baked foolish dreams, but she had a place here and people who needed her. It had been enough before Linc, and it would be so again. She'd make sure of it.

Families came in all shapes and sizes. These dear, kind souls were part of hers now, and she wouldn't let useless longings for a man who found her wanting in some way she didn't understand distract her from caring for those who did want her, who did have need of her.

Palo Verde was her new home, she resolved then and there. Even if Aunt Prudie recovered her strength and didn't require her help at the café, she could still make a difference. Maybe it wasn't the life she'd dreamed of, with the white picket fence and a man who loved her and gave her the babies she'd wanted so badly.

Linc Garner hadn't been that man, but he'd never promised to be. He'd comforted her through the darkest of nights and let her release the tears that ate into her heart like acid.

If her foolish heart had flirted with a dream of more, well, it wouldn't be the first time.

But she was through with that dream. Her life lay elsewhere. She would not have those babies or that man.

And someday, if she just kept putting one foot in front of the other, it would hurt less.

CHAPTER TWELVE

LINC SAT at the massive mahogany desk he would always consider his father's and rubbed the bridge of his nose as he stared at the screen of his laptop.

Rows and rows of numbers, all carefully arranged and crunched within an inch of their lives—

All pointing to the same, inescapable solution: no matter what Ivy dreamed she could make happen, tourism wasn't the answer. Palo Verde's survival depended upon growth. Growth depended upon industry wanting to be there, creating jobs. But there were fifty small towns much more accessible to Fort Worth to which industry would flock. Industry demands a workforce, and Palo Verde's had dwindled to almost nothing. Most of the people left in town were beyond retirement age.

Except for Ivy, who, ball of energy though she was, was only one woman.

He'd had an idea, though, that just might work: turn the scenic beauty around Palo Verde into an asset. Make the area a place to retire, to enjoy the slower, sweeter life of yesterday. Create an enclave that would draw the big money. Everything followed the money. Residents with bigger wallets, more expensive shops poised to pluck the bills from them.

More expensive shops could afford higher rents. Higher rents would soon attract investors…investors who wouldn't give a damn about Carl Thompson. Expensive rents that would drive Lora Lee back into retirement—

Linc's fist crashed down on the arm of his father's obscenely expensive leather chair.

Why was he still trying to figure out solutions for Ivy's dream? He'd promised to marry Betsey, and thus Betsey's need for the money from the buildings would be gone. Over time, the rents could go toward repairs. The buildings would be saved from the need to be sold. Ivy would be saved, too.

But she wouldn't be his. Not ever.

For the hundredth time in the past three-and-a-half weeks, Linc's hand hovered over the telephone. He'd long ago memorized the phone numbers at the café, at Ivy's little cottage. Just to hear her voice for a second…just to hear Carl complaining, Prudie giving him hell—

But Carl wouldn't be there yet. The latest report the home health agency had sent to him with an invoice said it would be a while yet before Carl could visit the café. He still had strength to build.

But he was giving the nursing staff hell, so he was clearly on the mend. Thinking of the cantankerous old man, Linc grinned. He'd had to pay a bonus to keep the nurses there, but it was money well spent if it prevented Ivy from burning the candle at both ends.

Ivy. It always came back to her. Often—all too often—she filled his thoughts, some odd memory of her. Dirt under her nails in the garden…kneading bread, her plump, pretty breasts jiggling slightly as her arms worked. Singing to Stevie in that soft, sweet voice. Ivy the sergeant major, exhorting the troops to fight to keep their town alive—

"Linc?"

His head jerked up. Betsey stood in the doorway, her face drawn and hollow. She spent most of her hours with his father; between himself and Betsey, a strange distance had fallen now that he'd acquiesced to his father's wish, though not to any definite plans for a wedding date.

He'd do what he'd promised, but he wasn't ready yet. That one fact surprised him as nothing else had in a long time—

Except for his once inexplicable attraction to Ivy Parker.

"Linc, you have to come now. He's—" Betsey's voice caught, and he realized that her eyes were red.

Guilt for thinking about Ivy at a time like this dogged him. With long strides, he closed the span between him and Betsey.

In the dark, silent room, he felt a boy again, shot through with fear. Memories breathed down his neck, sat on his shoulders...memories of the dark, terrifying days after his mother died, when he and Garner crept through the silence, staying together for courage, unnoticed by everyone—especially the man who now lay in the bed, his breath coming hard.

Linc shook off the boy whose world had shattered so long ago. He was a man now. The man of the house, heir to what was left of all his father had built.

And he, Linc? What had he built? He had no loved ones in his life, no one whose smile superseded a day's waiting tasks, the demands of fortune-seeking.

For a second, Ivy's laughing blue eyes danced into his vision. Feeling the traitor, he banished them.

Linc stepped up to his father's bedside, looking down at the hand lying so still on the covers. That hand had seldom touched him, either in anger or in love. Since he'd made his promise, Linc had visited this room every day, hoping that at last they would talk, would find a way to peace, but his father had retreated into silence, beyond a son's need for connection.

A great dark void yawned inside Linc, and his heart creaked with old aches.

Betsey leaned against him, her head resting against his chest. He tightened an arm around her, but it didn't help. She and he were separate in their grief; just as she filled nothing inside him, neither, he knew somehow, did he fill the empty spaces inside her. He had loved her once, and he had clung to that memory of love for many years, but now he saw that it was a dead love. They were an old item, a piece of the past not yet laid to rest in order to move on.

And now he could not. He had made a promise to a dying man for the sake of a brother who should still be alive.

Ivy hovered there, just out of range, an oasis that would always beckon but one he would never reach.

Oh, Ivy… Still, the thought of her comforted.

So in the best tradition of what he somehow knew Ivy would do, he reached for his father's hand…papery and frail.

"Dad…" Linc's voice faltered. He tried to clear

his throat past the sudden obstruction. "I understand."

His father opened his eyes for a second and stared into his. "Garner...Betsey..." The fierce eagle returned long enough to extract his promise.

Then Edward Lincoln Galloway II closed his eyes and breathed out one last, long, sighing breath.

Betsey gripped Linc's shirt in her fist and sobbed against his chest.

His own eyes were dry. The last of his family was gone, leaving him only this final chance to mend what had gone so wrong.

Betsey wasn't like his mother, didn't have Ivy's bottomless well of love. Maybe he didn't love her, but he could be good to her, could care for her as promised. Take up where his brother and father had left off.

It was the life he knew, after all. The other was only a boy's dream.

But he would go his father one better, by God he would.

One day he might have children.

His children, he would love. With everything in him.

IVY WALKED UP Carl's porch steps and knocked softly at the door with one free hand. In the other, she held another pie of Carl's favorite apple. He often napped in the afternoons, and she didn't want to wake him, but she hoped his grandson Jeff would hear her knock.

The door opened. Jeff smiled. "Hey, Ivy. Come on in." He sniffed. "Wow, what's that? Apple pie?" He rubbed his flat belly. "I have no idea how Granddad hasn't gained fifty pounds, eating your cooking."

Skimming just under six feet and very near her age, Jeff Thompson resembled Carl in few ways, especially personality. He was always cheerful, always eager to learn something new. He'd offered to help Ivy do any research she needed for her business plan, and she thought she might take him up on it. He'd told her all manner of wonders he could find on the Internet and even offered to set up a computer system for her while he was in town.

Ivy didn't think she was ready for a computer, but perhaps he could help her find the name and physical location of the real person behind the post office box to which they all sent their rent.

She'd spent almost a month burying her head in the café, experimenting with new recipes for the menu, making all of Carl's favorites. Instead of sleeping, she put up wallpaper and stripped the wood floors. She was even contemplating opening at night, just to escape from her thoughts, from the way the world seemed to have turned gray and lifeless. Even her appetite had suffered.

She kept going from one day to the next, ignoring the business plan that, every time she thought of it, brought memories of Linc.

But she knew she couldn't hide forever. She'd promised this town a solution, and it was only the native kindness and good manners of the merchants that kept them from bringing up her lack of follow-through. If Carl were back on his feet, he'd scold her good.

And she'd deserve it. Time to come out of hiding.

She smiled at Jeff, who'd made it clear that his interest didn't extend only to helping her with computers. "I'll make you a pie of your own as partial payment for a favor I'd like to ask."

His brown eyes lit. "Anything."

Ivy had to look away from his eagerness. She busied herself uncovering the pie and rummaging through Carl's kitchen drawers to find a knife. "You say there are amazing things you can find on the Internet."

"I could show you right now—"

Ivy turned and shook her head. "I'm afraid I need to get back, but I wonder if you could try to track down some information for me. Most of the merchants, including Aunt Prudie, make their rent payments to a corporation with only a post office box. These buildings need a lot of repairs, but the landlord isn't answering my letters, and I've promised the others that I'll go see him or her, but I don't know how to find out the name of a real person and the address where he or she is located."

"Piece of cake," he said, rubbing his hands. "Or pie, as it may be." He grinned at her. "I'll have it for you this afternoon. Tonight at the latest."

"Really? It's that easy? Please don't go to a lot of trouble."

"For a certified computer nerd like me, it's not hard work." Jeff winked and grinned. "And I'm going out of my mind sitting around here, waiting for Granddad to wake up and bitch."

She wanted to tell him that he didn't look like a nerd, that his clean, wholesome all-American appearance would attract a lot of women, she was sure. But she didn't want to encourage him to think that she could be included in that group. Her heart had a long way to go to be ready for any man. Linc had seen to that.

Linc. She sighed. When would he stop popping into her mind at odd moments?

"Big sigh," Jeff noted. "Want to tell me what's behind it?"

Ivy shook her head. "It's nothing, really. Just been a long day. I'd better get back, but please give Carl a kiss for me."

Jeff laughed. "I love Granddad a lot, but I think I'll let you do that for yourself. I'll tell him you requested it, though."

Ivy chuckled, and it felt good. She'd laughed much too little in the past few weeks. Despite her best intentions, she was just going through the motions, and she knew it.

Time for that to end. "Do you have my number for when you get the information?"

"Yep," he said, patting his chest. "Engraved on my heart." Then he grinned.

Ivy grinned back, feeling better than she had in days.

AUNT PRUDIE SETTLED into her chair. "That's not much of a supper," she pointed out.

"I'm not very hungry tonight," Ivy responded.

"You haven't been hungry much lately." Her great-aunt peered closely at her, scowling. "I've seen better-looking corpses."

Ivy had to laugh. "Thanks a lot." She picked up her fork and took a bite of the King Ranch chicken she'd made, chewing slowly. The queasy feeling was probably just hunger. She'd be fine after a few bites.

Two bites later, she knew she was wrong. She laid down her fork and pressed one hand to her stomach.

"And I told that boy he'd better not let Carl—" Aunt Prudie broke off. "Ivy, honey, there's not a speck of color in your face. Are you—"

Ivy bolted for the bathroom.

A few minutes later, she sat on the bathroom floor, letting Aunt Prudie wipe her face with a wet cloth. "You're not feeling sick, are you?" Ivy asked. "Was it my cooking?"

Aunt Prudie considered her for a moment, her china-blue eyes scrutinizing every inch. "No, I'm feeling fine, and I ate much more than you did. Is this why you're losing weight? How often has this happened?"

Ivy closed her eyes as the cool cloth did its magic. "I haven't had much appetite lately," she admitted. "Nothing sits well on my stomach, but this is the first time such a thing has happened."

Aunt Prudie's eyes turned tender. "Honey, I was up late the night that Carl got hurt. I saw Linc carry you into the house. I kept my mouth shut because it was your business, but I'm wondering now if you took proper precautions?"

"Proper pre—" Ivy's mind shut down, just shut down flat in the face of the enormity of what Aunt Prudie was suggesting.

"Are you telling me that you couldn't be pregnant?" Aunt Prudie asked.

Pregnant. Ivy put her hand over her mouth to keep from saying the word out loud, so fierce was the joy that struck her. She went blind momentarily from the incandescence of it, the sheer, wild rapture of the idea, the absolute—

Terror. Oh God. She bent double, arms clasping around her middle as if to hold the precious life inside. Logic told her she needed a pregnancy test, that there could be any manner of dire reasons that food revolted her.

But her heart leaped straight up in the air and clicked its heels. That night, that wonderful, glorious night when her tears had flowed, she'd been cleansed...her old sorrow had finally broken its bonds and been washed away by the salty river of her tears.

Linc had given her that. He'd held her while she cried, while tears too long denied had been the fertile rain to water the seed of a new life. She knew it, suddenly knew it deep in her bones, deep as the rush of her heart's blood.

"Honey, are you all right?" Aunt Prudie asked.

Her vision swept clean of the past, Ivy fixed her eyes on her future, a future that was now so bright and new. "Oh, yes," she said, grasping Prudie's hand. "Oh, yes...I couldn't be better." Her heart begged pardon from a God on whom she'd just about given up. *Thank You. Oh, thank You.*

"But what about Linc? How will you let him know?"

For a moment, her aunt's question didn't quite sink in.

Then Linc's face asserted itself in her memory, and a wave of sadness assaulted her. She thought of his first awkward handling of Stevie, the way he'd graduated to holding the baby closer, tucking her into those same strong arms that had given Ivy shelter on a night when darkness had overwhelmed her.

You'd be such a good father, Linc. A little practice needed, maybe, but—

She couldn't stand to think that he might never know his child. Perhaps Jeff could help her find him, too. Now she wished she'd written down the license number of his old truck. But such impulses to security just weren't in her nature.

Then she realized that Aunt Prudie was still waiting for an answer. "What? I'm sorry, I forgot the question."

Aunt Prudie smiled. "You're sure, aren't you."

Ivy nodded, smiling back. "I'll get a test, but yes...somehow I just feel it."

"So how will you inform Linc was my question."

Ivy's throat filled. "I hope I can, but I know nothing about him. He never wanted to talk about himself." She gripped Prudie's hands in hers and squeezed. She couldn't dodge forever the loss it would be to her and the baby both if they never found Linc, but right now, the sheer outrageous beauty of this discovery had her floating high, filled with confidence beyond measure.

"Even if I never find him, this baby will have all the love in the world, I promise you that. She'll never wonder if she's loved or wanted." Tears blurred her vision. "Oh, Auntie, I'm so happy—" When Aunt Prudie's arms tightened around her, Ivy burrowed into the comfort, smiling at a world that had suddenly flipped all the lights on.

I mean it, baby girl—or boy, I don't care which. I'll love you so much you'll be fine, even if we can't find your daddy.

Aunt Prudie patted her back and rocked her. "I know you will, sweetheart. No one loves better than you. No one."

IN THE PAUSE between breakfast and lunch the next day, Ivy turned over her apron to Aunt Prudie and a mystified Mabel with a promise to be back in a flash. She zipped down the road to Mineral Wells to the nearest drugstore and bought a pregnancy test. She held it on her lap all the way home, smiling like a loon. Grinning at the mere sight of a summer flower, of a child at play.

Alone in her cottage, she approached the test with all the solemnity and ceremony of a royal coronation. For a moment, she stood stock-still with the unused test strip in her hand, a dart of fear daring to rock her certainty.

But unlike most unwed mothers, the fear was not that the test would be positive. She wanted this child more than she wanted the sun to rise in the morning. And despite all caution and good sense, she wanted a child of Linc's body as well as her own.

Even if she never saw him again.

At that thought, the bubble of her joy sank toward the ground. Yes, she wanted this baby, missing father or not, tough road ahead notwithstanding. She wasn't afraid of the work or the burden she would carry alone. Of course she would rather be raising this baby with its father by her side, but doing it alone felt no burden at all at the moment. The weight on her joy was a longing to share this news with Linc, to complete a real, live family.

But he might not welcome the news. He might have a wife stashed away or be an escaped convict or any number of scenarios. He was the most intensely private man she'd ever met; he might like his life alone.

Ivy stared at the test strip, too thin and fragile for the import it carried, and for an instant, fear won the day.

Then she shook her head. She'd never found it worthwhile to sit on the sidelines and wait. Better to face the news, whatever it was, and get started on dealing with it.

HUGGING THE SECRET to herself, Ivy had practically danced her way through the lunch rush. Mabel's curiosity was a force to be reckoned with; she'd refused to leave for the day until Ivy spilled her guts.

So Ivy spilled. Mabel laughed and started planning a baby shower. Ivy had sworn her to secrecy; Mabel had promised, and Ivy thought she'd keep that promise.

But in truth, Ivy was the one having trouble keeping the news to herself. She wanted to sing it from the courthouse cupola, wanted to take out an ad in the Palo Verde paper. When Jeff walked in while Ivy was mopping the floor, dancing with the mop, discretion had never come harder. But she couldn't tell Jeff until she'd told Carl first; Carl would never forgive her.

"Hi," Jeff said. "You look happy."

Ivy grinned. "I am."

"You look good happy." He peered at her.

"Really good. May I ask what's brought the change?"

Ivy's smile vanished. "Oh, Jeff, I wish I could tell you, but I can't just yet." Then she smiled again. "But I promise I'll tell you soon. Maybe later today, in fact."

He nodded. "Good enough. You ready for the identity of Simon Legree?"

"You got it? Already?"

Jeff cast her a sideways glance. "I'm actually embarrassed it took me this long. There's quite a trail to follow."

Ivy parked the mop in its bucket and wiped her hands on her apron. "How do you know how to do it?"

Jeff wrinkled his nose. "Well, Granddad would tell you that if I spent as much time trying to find a good woman as I do wandering the Internet, I'd be married and have five kids by now." He shrugged. "I've been keeping my eyes open. The right woman just hadn't come along."

The intensity of his gaze worried Ivy. Especially now, she couldn't let him fall prey to misconceptions about her. "Jeff, I—" She fell silent, unsure what to say.

"Look, Ivy, I think you should know how I feel—"

"I'm pregnant," she blurted out. *Sorry, Carl.*

"What?" He goggled. "What did you say?"

"I'm pregnant. That's why I look so happy. I can't have you thinking that we could—"

"You're not married." He frowned.

Ivy's back stiffened. "No. I'm not. Not that it's any business of yours."

Jeff glanced away, then back, rubbing the back of his neck with one hand. "I'm sorry. That's not an accusation. I just meant—" He sighed. "Who is he, Ivy?"

The thought occurred again to Ivy that Jeff might be able to help her find Linc. Just as quickly, she discarded it. Not yet, anyway. The situation was already awkward enough.

"It doesn't matter. He won't be part of the picture."

"That sonofa—" Jeff's frown darkened. "Why not?"

"Jeff," Ivy said, placing one hand on his arm, "it's all right. He doesn't know. I just found out myself."

"Where is he?"

She tried to smile. "I have no idea—" At his swift, vile curse, she patted his arm again. "But it doesn't matter. I want this baby very much. I'll be fine."

"Ivy, you can't—" Jeff shook his head and grinned. "Hell, you probably can do it by yourself, but do you honestly think that's the best thing for the child? Kids need fathers, too, you know.''

Ivy remembered the man who'd abandoned her and her sisters. ''I realize that,'' she said. ''But I'm not going in search of a man to be this child's father.''

''You wouldn't have to look far.'' Once more his eyes were intent.

For a moment, Ivy thought she wouldn't be able to speak because of the lump in her throat. She raised her hand to his chest. ''Jeff, if you're offering what I think you're offering, that's very sweet.'' She smoothed out a wrinkle in his shirt, then lifted her gaze to his. ''But we barely know each other. I like you, and I'd welcome your friendship, but I've been married before and I'm not eager to enter into another relationship until I'm sure it's right. I made a big mistake before—'' She blinked back the threatening tears. ''I won't do that again. I wish I knew where my baby's father was, but I don't, and I'm just going to make the best of it. I'm going to concentrate all my resources on growing this baby and bringing it into this world.''

She looked up at Jeff, so close to her own age but so innocent. The sudden image of Linc's troubled gray eyes intervened, eyes filled with unnamed sorrows. He was so alone. In that moment, the need for him pierced her very soul.

Ivy wrapped her arms around herself and tightened her fingers in the fabric of her dress, swallowing hard. "Thank you for caring about me. I'll be fine, I promise." She cleared her throat, then spoke briskly. "Now, tell me about this elusive landlord. I'm going to need to make a trip to Dallas very soon." More than ever, she wanted to secure a future for this town—and for herself. She would sink roots here in Palo Verde. This baby might never have a father, but it would have a whole town to stand in its father's stead.

"If you change your mind, Ivy—" Jeff's brown eyes reflected his concern.

"Thank you, more than I can say." She smiled and patted his arm again. "Now, Mr. Magician, tell me how to find Simon Legree."

CHAPTER THIRTEEN

"LINC?"

He looked up at the sound of Betsey's voice, surprised to see her here in his father's downtown Dallas office. With the familiarity of many visits, she smiled dismissal at his father's secretary, Mrs. Dobson, who'd jumped at the chance to return to work. After thirty years, her knowledge of his father's business affairs was invaluable in winding up the estate.

"Hi," he said to Betsey, brushing a kiss of welcome on her cheek. "What's up? I didn't expect you here."

In the wake of his father's death, it was as though the air had leaked out of a balloon inflated for too long. Garner's tragic death, then the devotion and energy Betsey had expended on his father in the last months had depleted her resources. She'd slept the better part of two days after the funeral, and Linc was glad for the respite he now suspected was drawing to a close.

He'd promised to marry her. He couldn't put it

off forever. He felt like a traitor even using those words. Betsey deserved better than a man who'd finally realized that the memory of love he'd carried around for years was just that—a memory. Not alive. Not growing. A boy's memory of the one who got away.

Then he had met Ivy Parker. Had caught a glimpse of a dream.

And now he had to forget her.

"I thought maybe—" Uncustomary nerves showed in the darting of her gaze, the tangling of her fingers. "I wondered if you had some time to talk about plans for the wedding."

"Bets, I'm sorry. I've just got so much to do here—the mess is worse than I'd realized." He gestured at the papers on top of the pile.

Her gaze lowered. "What are those?" She pointed at the photographs he'd had taken of the buildings in Palo Verde. This morning he'd received a purchase offer for them from feelers he'd put out before he'd ever paid his visit.

"This—" he indicated "—is what's left after Garner got through gambling. It's your legacy— some run-down buildings in a town that's on its last legs."

The minute the harsh words were out of his mouth, he wanted to recall them. This mess wasn't Betsey's fault, and it shouldn't grate on him that she was so ignorant and helpless. "I'm sorry. I'm just so damn angry at the waste."

"You're exhausted," she said. "You had a nice life carved out for yourself, and then your father dumped all of this, including me, on your shoulders. I'll bet you wish he'd never contacted you."

He heard both a surprising courage and the chagrin in her voice. "He didn't dump you on me. I'm glad to help you, Bets." That much was true.

"Well, I don't like being a burden. I should have been a more modern woman, had a career. I followed my mother's example and left everything about our finances in Garner's hands." Her voice held a bitter edge. "I don't want to be helpless anymore, Linc. I want you to explain exactly where things stand. It's time I learned how to take care of myself."

"I'll take care of you, Bets."

She shot him a rueful smile. "You may have to—I may be hopeless at this." Then she straightened. "But I want to try. I need to try. I hid behind Daddy, then Garner and Edward. I don't want to hide behind you." She nodded at the pictures. "So why don't you start by explaining about what Garner left me?"

Linc studied her for a moment, seeing a new resolve in her. Admiration stirred and gave him his first sense of hope. Maybe he didn't love her with the hot rush of a young man's infatuation, but perhaps here was something they could build on.

So he picked up the pictures and began to explain what he'd learned about Palo Verde. She asked good questions, reminding him that though she might know little about business, she was an intelligent woman. Then he picked up the fax that had come that morning and explained its terms.

"It doesn't seem like much money for that many buildings," she observed. "Am I wrong?"

"No. But fixing up those buildings would be throwing good money after bad. You'd never get your money back."

"So you think I should sell them?"

No. From deep inside him came the answer. He'd tried unsuccessfully to dismiss the people of Palo Verde from his mind, to discuss this as a simple matter of business.

But Palo Verde wouldn't go away.

"There's one other option," he said, "but you wouldn't get the money quickly."

"What is it?"

"You could sell them to me, but I have to free up some of my capital first, and it might take a few more weeks."

"You?" Betsey looked up from perusing the fax, startled. "But you said it's a bad deal. Why would you want to buy them?"

Linc's mind raced as he tried to figure out how to explain what he didn't understand himself—

"Mr. Galloway, you have visitors." Mrs. Dobson appeared in the doorway before he could respond.

"Visitors?" He frowned. "I wasn't expecting anyone. Who are they?"

"I don't know two of their names, but the person who's most insistent upon seeing you says her name is Ivy Parker. Shall I show her in?"

Linc's mind blanked out in shock. He was silent so long that Betsey stepped in.

"I'd love to meet this Ivy Parker," she said. "Please show her in, Mrs. Dobson."

Mrs. Dobson looked at Linc for direction.

The best he could do was a nod.

"MR. GALLOWAY will see you now," the older woman said, but her frown told Ivy what she already knew—that her attire, though it was her best dress, marked her as someone who didn't belong here. The floors were glossy parquet overlaid with a huge Oriental rug in shades of burgundy and forest green. English hunting prints lined the walls, each in a thick gold frame. The imposing antique furniture was walnut and appeared genuine. Over it all presided a dignified and elegant silver-haired woman.

If this Mr. Galloway was half as intimidating as his secretary, she was already doomed. But Ivy Parker wasn't a quitter. She pressed one hand to her stomach to soothe her jitters. She hadn't been able to eat breakfast for the nerves. She had more than ever on the line now. She had to sell this business plan that they'd slaved over for a week.

She started across the carpet, realizing she was walking alone. "Come with me," she whispered to Lora Lee and Jeff. "Please."

Both rose to their feet. Ivy felt better just knowing there were friends by her side. She followed the secretary down the hall, rehearsing her first words. *I'm sorry for your loss, Mr. Galloway.* The secretary had explained that the owner of these offices had passed away recently and that it was his son she would be seeing.

"In here…" the secretary gestured.

Beyond the woman's fingertips, Ivy saw a huge office with thick carpet, more expensive furniture and an entire wall of windows. The sun poured in through them, casting the two people in the room into shadows. She blinked against the light and entered the room, trying to make out their faces.

The man didn't move, but the woman—a stunning brunette—crossed the carpet. She offered her hand. "Ms. Parker, I've been hearing about you," she said. "I'm Linc's fiancée, Betsey Galloway."

"Betsey, don't—" said a voice Ivy still heard in her dreams. She couldn't seem to move or think as she stared at the hand before her and struggled to lift hers to meet it.

It couldn't be. *Fiancée?* That voice. It couldn't be—

The man moved out of shadows and walked toward her with an all-too-familiar stride—

"Ivy—" he said.

Lora Lee gasped. Jeff stirred beside her.

Ivy struggled to find her voice. *Linc?* Linc's fiancée? *The son of the owner,* the woman had said.

The sound of a heart breaking should be crisp, brittle. All Ivy felt was the too-sudden plummet. The dull, sickening thud as her hopes crashed to earth. As foolish dreams died.

Betrayed. Again. By a man she'd thought she loved.

The colors in the room pulsated, suddenly too bright, too painful, her head pounding, her breath locking in her throat—

Ivy's legs collapsed beneath her, and the world was dark.

SHE WAS THERE, right there before him, more beautiful than ever, horror dawning in her eyes.

Linc had been searching for the words to explain

over his own shock, when Ivy's face lost all color and she slid to the floor.

His own heart stopped. "Ivy!" he shouted, leaping forward. He caught her as she fell.

"Mrs. Dobson," he barked. "Call 911—" Thank God they weren't in Palo Verde and could get expert medical care fast. That was his first thought in the noise all around him.

His trembling fingers searched for a pulse. When he felt it, strong and sure, relief rolled over him in waves. He bowed his head over Ivy, drawing her close. "Thank God," he gasped.

"Linc?" Betsey asked. "What's going on?"

"Who the hell are you?" The man who'd been at Ivy's side snapped at Linc. "Get away from her."

A sound very like a growl issued from Linc's throat. He met the younger man's gaze with a clear warning of his own.

"Linc, let me see her." Lora Lee Johnson knelt with difficulty beside Ivy's too-still body.

"What's wrong with her?" he said helplessly. "Mrs. Dobson," he shouted. "Where the hell are the paramedics?"

Lora Lee's hand clasped his forearm. "Linc, listen to me."

He saw sympathy warring with distrust. "She's hurt. What happened?"

Lora Lee's voice was kind. "I don't think she's hurt. I think she simply fainted."

He studied Ivy, saw the dark circles beneath her eyes. Felt her light and insubstantial in his arms. "She's lost weight," he accused. "She's been working on that damn business plan, hasn't she. Why isn't she eating? Hasn't anyone been paying attention—"

Ivy stirred.

"She's pregnant," the other man shouted. "Are you the lousy bastard who abandoned her to have your baby alone?"

Linc heard Betsey's gasp, but for the second time this morning, he lost all power of speech. He glanced over at Lora Lee, seeing confirmation in her eyes. And condemnation.

Ivy's lids began to flutter. Her chest rose on a deep inhalation.

He stared at the woman in his arms, stunned. Assaulted by terror: him, a father? By joy so huge and deep it threatened to burst his chest. *Ivy. Carrying my baby.* He didn't doubt for a minute it was his, remembering a night so rich and rare that it was fitting they should have created a child. A child. *His* child. Linc recalled watching Ivy singing to Stevie. His child's mother, a woman born to the role—

Long, dark lashes lifted to reveal beautiful blue

eyes soft with pleasure at the sight of him. "Linc," Ivy said, reaching up to stroke his face.

Gratitude rushed over him. He stared at her, the words *my child* rolling around in his head. "My baby?" His voice faltered. "Ivy—"

"Linc, what's going on?" Betsey's voice snapped him back into the real world. "What's the meaning of this? How can you promise to marry me when you and she—"

"Oh—" Ivy stiffened in his arms. Linc held her close. She began to struggle against him. "Let me go."

"Ivy, don't. Be careful, you might hurt—"

She went instantly still, but he might as well have been holding a block of ice. Ivy wouldn't meet his eyes.

"You heard the lady," the man with her insisted.

"Who the hell are you?"

"He's Carl's grandson, Jeff." Lora Lee explained. "Let her go, Linc." She drew Ivy from his arms.

Ivy glanced past Linc to where Betsey stood. "If it's any consolation," she said without expression, "he lied to me, too." She put her hand out for the younger man to help her rise, then extended her assistance to Lora Lee.

On her way out, she paused in front of Betsey.

"He lied to a lot of people." Avoiding any glance in Linc's direction, she spoke to Carl's grandson. "I'd like to leave now. This visit was pointless—" Her voice broke.

He had to get her attention. "Ivy, we have to talk," he demanded. "That's my child. I take care of my obligations."

Ivy froze but didn't turn. "That's the difference between us, Linc. I consider this baby a joy, not an obligation." At the doorway, she faced him. "I don't need your help, Linc, whoever you are. I won't accept it. I'll raise this baby on my own."

Linc heard noise down the hall and realized that the paramedics had arrived. "They're here. Sit down, Ivy, and let them check you over."

"Jeff," Ivy said. "Please tell them that I'm fine and won't be needing any help."

"Don't be stupid, Ivy. Let them examine you," Linc insisted.

She tilted her chin in that stubborn way he'd seen often. "I've already been stupid. I won't make that mistake again." She gave him her back. "Jeff, I'll see them, but not in here. Not with—him."

"Ivy…" He cast about for something to keep her here. His gaze landed on the fax. "The buildings—I've got an offer here from someone who wants to buy them."

She stopped in her tracks. "Good. Perhaps it's someone who has the decency to answer my letters."

Enraged that she refused to deal with him, Linc told her the rest. "He's hoping to get a contract to build a minimum-security prison facility outside Palo Verde and wants to use them for cheap office space."

He saw a tremor shake her frame, heard Lora Lee's gasp of horror. "I can help you, Ivy. Stay here and talk to me." Then he held out the carrot. "It won't have to hurt your café. I have a great location in Dallas picked out, where you can move it. You can make a mint."

At last, Ivy met his gaze, but her expression dripped pity and contempt. "I'd sooner talk to the devil himself," she said. "I don't care about your location, and I don't want any more of your help—" Her voice shook, but she didn't falter. "I'm going to fight you on this, Linc, and I'm going to win."

With a bearing that would have done a queen proud, she walked away.

Taking all the light in the room with her.

CHAPTER FOURTEEN

WHEN THE REPORTER from the *Fort Worth Star-Telegram* called first thing the next morning, Linc had to tip his hat to Ivy for possessing far more sophistication than he'd have credited. When the *Dallas Morning News* chimed in before noon, wanting to know why a wealthy man had it in for a small town so much that he'd sell his family's heritage, he'd gotten his back up and barely resisted saying something not fit to print.

When two radio stations wanted interviews and the first television film crew showed up, Linc got mad. He spent the day dodging reporters and fielding offers to buy the buildings, in between comforting Betsey after the *Morning News* gossip columnist had called her, wanting to drag Garner's death into the picture and digging for how Betsey felt about her former brother-in-law-turned-fiancé knocking up Palo Verde's own Joan of Arc.

But when he turned on the evening local news and saw tears gather in Ivy's eyes after a reporter introduced her as an abandoned unwed mother, it was the last straw. It didn't matter if Ivy had brought this firestorm upon them. No one was going to take a cheap shot at the woman who still haunted his nights and tangled up his dreams.

He'd phoned Ivy over and over, but she'd refused his calls. He'd tried talking to Aunt Prudie, but the older woman hung up on him. Lora Lee was slightly less obdurate, but not much. And meanwhile, damn it, that grandson of Carl's had his arm around Ivy every time she was interviewed.

He—the devil himself, as she'd called him— was going to Palo Verde, and Ivy Parker was going to talk to him if he had to kidnap her to do it.

But first, he had to tell Betsey.

HE FOUND HER in her room, packing. "Where are you going?"

"One of my friends has extended several invitations to visit her in New York since Garner died." She didn't look up from the blouse she was folding. "I think now might be a good time to get away. I need to figure out what to do next."

"I'll have this mess straightened out in a day or two. You don't have to worry about anything."

Her hands stilled. "I've hidden from life—real life—too long. It was easy to get caught up in caring for Edward after Garner…died. Too easy. Too convenient. Now there's nothing to hide behind.''

"I'm here, Bets. I said I'd take care of you."

She looked up, sorrow in her eyes. "Don't, Linc."

"Don't what?" The ground beneath him felt shaky.

"Don't pretend anymore that I'm anything but a duty. If you were still in love with me, there'd be wedding plans in the works."

"There've been a lot of loose ends to deal with…settling the estate—"

"You're not going to dodge the point. I saw how you looked at her." Her voice was fond and tender. "You're in love with her, aren't you?" she asked. "Even if she wasn't having your baby, she's the one you really want."

"Bets, I promised—"

She shook her head, her expression wistful. "We just can't seem to get it right, can we? I did love you back then, you know. You were so exciting, so alive, but you scared me to death with all your fire and fury. The air always seemed ready to burst into flames when you were in the room." She clasped the blouse to her chest. "I think I knew even then that you were too much for me."

"I wasn't. I wanted you so much. When you went back home—" He stopped, remembering. "I wanted to hate you it hurt so damn bad. But I couldn't. I loved you.''

They both heard the past tense.

"I'm sorry I wasn't braver," Betsey told him. "I'm just not like her."

And there she was. Ivy, right in the room with them. "She's not my type," he said, though by now he knew it didn't matter in the least.

Betsey laughed then, the first honest laugh he'd heard from her since he'd returned. "I know, but I suspect she may be exactly what you need. She's small in stature, but she's obviously got a lion's heart." Amusement slow-danced with sorrow. "You have your work cut out for you, trying to win her back. I'm almost sorry I won't be around to watch the fireworks."

He saw her eyes fill. "Bets, I don't know what to tell you. I don't want to hurt you. I never expected to—" He broke off before he could say it. *Fall in love.* "I'll make sure you're taken care of, I promise. It's the least I can do."

She brushed at her tears and busied herself placing the blouse in her suitcase. "I'm tired of being a burden. If I had taken more interest in what was going on, maybe Garner wouldn't have felt so much pressure." Her voice trembled. "Maybe he'd still be alive."

Linc waved off her guilt, too sure of his own.

"If I hadn't turned my back on him, I would have seen what was happening. Could have helped fix what was so wrong. I could have stopped him before he—" The grief for his brother that Linc had held at bay for weeks now rolled over him in a punishing wave.

Betsey took his hand, then leaned in to him. "You can't blame yourself, Linc. Edward set the tone for all of us long ago. He cast you out with nothing, told you never to return. He placed too much on Garner's shoulders and refused to see that Garner couldn't carry the load. And I played the princess in the tower, happy as long as my wardrobe was full of pretty gowns." She pressed her forehead in to his shoulder. "Poor Garner. I did love him, you know."

"Yeah," Linc murmured. For so many years, he'd forgotten how much he'd loved his brother. He'd have to find a way to live with knowing that he'd remembered too late.

In their shared grief, they clung together, their embrace one of family, though—not of lovers. Inside Linc, something gave way. The life he'd once wished for, the ambitions to show his father how wrong he'd been, the dream of Betsey he'd clung to all these years—all broke loose from the moorings in his heart where he'd lashed them tightly for fifteen years.

Fear claimed their place. He could never go back, and the future lay empty before him.

"I don't know what I'll do next, Linc, and I'll appreciate any help you're willing to give." Betsey hugged him once, then stepped back. "But I can't marry you. You deserve better than that, and I do, too. You should go after her."

Go after her. Ivy was furious with him and so hurt. He'd done that. That malice had played no part didn't matter; he'd hurt the one person in the world who least deserved it, the person most deserving of—

Love. Linc stared at nothing and reeled from the discovery. He loved Ivy Parker. Ivy Parker was having his baby. She would love that baby the way no child ever had been, regardless of what she felt for the baby's father.

He wanted Ivy to love him, too. He wanted the chance to cherish them both.

Hope rose like the first faint fingers of dawn. Winning Ivy wasn't going to be easy, judging from the fury in Lora Lee's voice, Aunt Prudie's refusal to speak to him; the whole town was probably madder than hell at him. But he'd fought a lot of battles since the day he'd been cast out on his own, and he'd won all the important ones.

He would win this time, too.

"Want some advice?" Betsey asked.

He nodded.

"Buying buildings isn't going to win her back. I don't think money means anything to her. If you really love her, you're going to have to do something you've avoided for a very long time."

"What's that?"

"You're going to have to bare your heart to her. Let her see inside you."

He knew she was right, but— "I'm not good at talking about things like that."

She smiled and kissed his cheek. "I know. But Linc, you feel things deeply. You wouldn't have stayed away so long if what happened here hadn't mattered. You've never let anything you wanted to accomplish stand in your way, except when it comes to your heart. You're just like your father."

"No, I'm nothing like him. I won't be." Then he remembered seeing himself in the mirror that morning at his father's bedside. He shoved his hands in his pockets and started to pace.

Betsey crossed to him, stopping him with one hand on his forearm. "Remember his regrets, Linc. He didn't know how to open his heart to you or Garner, and he lost you both. Don't make his mistakes. Your desire to take care of Ivy and your baby is good, but it means more than providing for them financially."

He wanted to care for them in all ways. He just

didn't know how to do it. "I can't even get her to speak to me. Plus, I have to separate her from that overgrown puppy who's always got his arm around her."

"I saw the way she looked at him and the way she looks at you. She may be furious with you, but that's your edge."

"How do you figure that?"

"Men." Betsey smiled, shaking her head. "Trust me, Linc. You don't feel furious with someone who doesn't matter. Now, you'd better hurry. You've got a mess to untangle, and the day's not getting any younger."

He started to leave, then returned to place his hands on her shoulders. "Bets—" he began.

She put the fingers of one hand over his mouth. "I'll be all right, Linc. I swear it. Just go, okay?"

His heart ached for her, and he wondered why it was that love chose odd partners, had lousy timing, was more inscrutable than any ancient soothsayer.

"I care about you, Bets," he whispered, kissing her on the forehead, like a brother. "I always will."

She closed her eyes, leaned against him for a second. "I know. Me, too." Then she pulled away and straightened visibly into the elegant socialite he'd met when he'd come back. But he could sense she was vulnerable and unsure.

Her voice revealed none of that, though. "Go," she said, strong and certain.

Linc couldn't figure out how to make things right or easy for her. So he simply nodded and left.

IVY PUNCHED ONE FIST into the dough on the breadboard, pretending it was the face of that nosy gossip columnist from Dallas. She'd thought she was ready for what she'd unleashed with her phone calls and letters to the media, but she'd never expected them to poke into her private life.

With strong, practiced fingers, she kneaded the soft mound, wishing she could take draw comfort from the tidbits the platinum, greedy-eyed columnist had dropped about how badly Linc's fiancée had handled the news of Ivy's pregnancy.

Why should his fiancée be upset? She had everything, including Linc. She was tall and stylish, her beauty breathtaking. She was every prom queen Ivy had ever watched from the sidelines, every football hero's girlfriend, lithe and lovely and utterly secure in her world. She and the Linc Ivy had seen in Dallas were perfectly suited, the golden modern couple on the rise.

How had the man in faded blue jeans seemed so real? The man who'd held her while she shed long-overdue tears, who'd gotten her coffee and held her hand when she was terrified Carl was dying…the man who'd made love to her with such tender passion—

He didn't exist. The man who'd touched her heart, who'd stolen her breath, was a gut-wrenching, mind-stealing lie.

Yet he'd given her the baby who was already her heart, her soul, her reason for existence, who was more essential to her than blood and bone.

Seeing Linc in Dallas had scared her to death. She didn't know that powerful figure in the perfectly tailored suit. If he would go to such lengths for some run-down old buildings, what would he do to possess his only child?

A shiver ran through Ivy. She had so little to bring to the battle should he want to fight her for custody. Her hands stilled on the dough.

Then she recalled the remote expression on his face when he'd first heard that she was pregnant. After a pause that seemed to last aeons, he'd made the respectable offer, but she could tell it was merely for form. Not a trace of emotion had crossed his face.

A twinge in her lower back had her straightening. At least he hadn't asked if she was sure the baby was his. For a moment, she wished she'd had the presence of mind to tell him the child *wasn't* his, but even if she hadn't been so shocked at meeting him, lying about something so important just wasn't in her.

"Ivy?" Aunt Prudie spoke from the doorway, surveying the profusion of breads in various stages of rising. "How long have you been here?"

Ivy looked away. "Not that long."

"You couldn't sleep again," Aunt Prudie accused. "Honey, you can't let this keep you from sleeping. That baby needs—"

"I know, Aunt Prudie. I do. I stayed in bed as long as I could." Shoving back dread, Ivy put special care into forming loaves from the mound of soft dough. "I'm trying. I swear I am."

"Oh, honey…this battle is taking too much out of you. You don't look good. You're exhausted. You can't be thinking of Palo Verde at a time like this. You have to focus on only one thing—this blessed child you're carrying."

"I know," Ivy whispered. "But this baby needs a home. I never had one, not really." Determination steadied her voice. "I'm going to see to it that this baby is never unsure about where she belongs."

"Halloo?" Mabel walked in from the back door, already tying her apron. She stopped and looked around, lifting one eyebrow at all the loaves.

"Don't start," Ivy warned. "I've already been chewed out."

Mabel and Aunt Prudie traded glances. Mabel shrugged. "I think I'll start the coffee."

Ivy realized she'd been here for three hours already. Rubbing her lower back, feeling exhaustion drift over her like a crippling fog, she wanted nothing more than to curl up in a corner and weep.

Instead, she formed the last loaf, then moved to the refrigerator. "Howard will be here soon, expecting his bacon and eggs."

Out of the corner of her eye, she saw Aunt Prudie mouthing something to Mabel.

"If you two have nothing better to do than gossip about me, you can just do it upstairs. I can handle things fine down here."

Mabel snorted. "A puff of wind could blow you over, girl. Howard and June won't be here for a bit. Why don't you go back to your place and nap a little?"

"I have a business to run," Ivy snapped. Instantly, she regretted her tone. "I'm sorry." She looked at both of them. "You're worried, and I appreciate that you care. I'll nap after the breakfast run, but for now..." She trailed off. "I need to work. It's the only thing that helps."

She could see protests forming on their lips and waited, suddenly much too tired to argue.

With relief and regret, she watched them move into their daily routine. When they were out of sight, she leaned her forehead against the refrigerator for a second.

Then she focused on the requirements of the day, the same way she'd gotten through so many days of the past year.

LINC DIDN'T KNOW WHY he'd expected everything to be changed when he drove into Palo Verde. To find that nothing was, that the same veil of genteel shabbiness still clothed the buildings downtown, brought an odd comfort. Driving up to Ivy's café, he had the unsettling feeling that he'd somehow come home, that welcome and respite lay inside those walls.

Pretty stupid, considering that he and Ivy were in a state of war, although conducted through intermediaries thus far.

He glanced around for news trucks, and was grateful to find them absent. Maybe he and Ivy were old news; maybe the worst of it was over. Maybe they could truly have the crucial conversation in private, the one where he explained about why he'd come to Palo Verde incognito, why he'd felt the need to—

Lie.

Admit it, buddy. You lied to her, pure and simple.

But he'd had a good reason. He'd been protecting Betsey, and how could he have imagined Ivy Parker, the diminutive amazon disguised as earth mother? How could he have known how she'd turn his ordered world upside down?

He parked his Jag in the only open slot, wondering yet again if he'd made a mistake coming here as the person he really was. Maybe if he'd driven the pickup again, she'd remember how they were together, how they'd been something incredible, how one night had glowed brighter than any field of stars.

He'd almost compromised and worn his old blue jeans. It wasn't as if he never wore them—he'd spent years wearing jeans most days and still donned them when it was time to relax, though he didn't relax all that often, he'd realized. But he'd decided that he owed it to Ivy to come to her honestly.

He climbed out of his car and stood there in slacks and a polo shirt, staring at the café. Just then, the front door opened and Howard and June Ledbetter emerged. Howard did a double take, started toward him with outstretched hand, then stopped. June glared at him and tugged on Howard's sleeve. With a look Linc couldn't read, Howard grasped his wife's elbow and walked in the other direction.

So that was the way the wind blew. Linc didn't know why it should hurt as much as it did.

He glanced at his watch. The breakfast rush wouldn't be quite over. Perhaps he should wait until—

He drew himself up short. There wasn't a good time for this. Maybe he'd be lucky and no one would pay much attention to his presence.

Only two seconds inside the café and he saw that he'd obviously forgotten too much about Palo Verde. Conversation ground to a halt. In less than a minute, the only sounds in the place were those coming from the kitchen. No one was eating. Everyone was staring at him as though Satan himself had just appeared.

In his life, Linc had surmounted cutthroat competitors and bikers wielding knives in seedy bars, and he'd never backed down. For the first time ever, he seriously considered turning around and walking away.

But just then, he caught a glimpse of Ivy's blond hair, and that was it. He couldn't take his eyes off her as she emerged from the kitchen.

Seeing her again was like having a punch leveled straight at his heart. She was so beautiful, in that unique way that made a man think of warm, cozy fires and hot, sultry nights, of puppies and kittens as much as lacy underwear on satin sheets.

She stopped in her tracks, her gaze frozen on his, and he realized that she was thinner than before, that shadows hollowed her cheeks and darkened her eyes.

Like a heat-seeking missile, he shot across the room and reached for her before he could even think. "What's wrong with you? Are you sick? Is the baby—?"

Ivy shrugged off his hold and stepped back. "What are you doing here?"

"Answer me," he snapped. "Is the baby all right?"

Confusion darted over her face. "Why do you care?"

His eyes widened. "Why do I care? It's my child."

She looked defiant. "You don't know that."

For a shocked second, he actually considered that the child might not be his. It didn't last. "No," he said, shaking his head. "You're not like that. You wouldn't go to another person's bed after we—"

Hectic color rose in her cheeks. "Why not? You did." With that, she whirled toward the kitchen.

Linc recoiled and almost let her get away. He grabbed her arm. "You don't understand," he began.

She didn't wait to hear. "I understand plenty,"

she spat. "You came here, you lied to all of us, you wormed your way into our confidence, and then you—" Her voice wavered as memories of that night rose in her eyes.

She tugged again, but he wouldn't let her go, afraid that if she got away from him, he'd never have another chance.

"Get your hands off her, Galloway." Carl's grandson grabbed Linc's arm and jerked hard.

Ivy slipped from Linc's grasp. Linc started after her. The next thing he knew, a fist came out of nowhere and slammed into his face.

Knocked back on his heels by the surprise blow, Linc still came up swinging. The tensions of the past several weeks coalesced into fury. Rubbed raw from Ivy's rejection, from his father's death, from trying to balance the demands of his old life with the pressures of the past, Linc took immense satisfaction in returning his attacker's blow. He hadn't been in a brawl since he was a teenager, but he hadn't forgotten how.

Shouts echoed around them, but he barely heard. He dodged a fist but toppled a stack of glassware, hardly noticing the splinters showering the floor. Balanced on the balls of his feet, he threw his body into the next blow.

Ivy's voice cut through the fracas. "Linc, stop— Jeff, no—"

Linc's heel slid on a carpet of glass. He lost his balance and fell backward into a body.

"Ivy—" Aunt Prudie cried.

Linc saw Ivy out of the corner of his eye and jerked in midair, trying to shift his weight—

Too late, he heard Ivy hit the floor and barely avoided falling on top of her. Her head hit hard.

In less than a breath, he'd scrambled to a crouch over her. "Ivy—oh God, Ivy, are you all right?"

Her eyes never even fluttered. He wanted to pick her up and race for help.

"Don't move her," Jeff warned.

"I know that," Linc snapped. "Call for an ambulance." Anguish burning through him like acid, he glanced at Aunt Prudie, unsure as he'd never been in his life. "They could take forever—" His fingers felt like fat sausages as he searched for a pulse. When he finally got it, he kept losing count. "Damn it."

Mabel knelt beside him, heedless of the glass scattered everywhere. "I used to be a practical nurse. Let me do it."

Linc moved back a little, scanning Ivy's body. Her skirt was rucked up high on her thighs. He reached to pull it down and spotted bright red staining the fabric beneath her.

A huge fist crushed the breath out of him.

"Oh, no," Prudie said. "Not again."

Linc's head jerked up. "What do you mean?"

"Ivy miscarried a baby last year."

"Oh God." Linc leaned over her. "Ivy—" He looked around. "Has somebody called the ambulance?" he roared.

"Already done," said a customer Linc had never seen. "They said they're close."

"Linc." Mabel touched his arm.

"Goddamn it, Mabel, we can't wait on them—"

Compassion warred with anger. "We don't have any choice." She looked over his shoulder. "We need to wrap her up and elevate her legs."

"It takes too long for them to get here," he shouted, heart tearing from his chest. "I can't lose her," he whispered. "She has to be all right. The baby—"

Linc felt a hand close over his shoulder. He looked up to see Carl. "Son, you got to do what's best for Ivy."

Linc bowed his head and battled back the sense of helplessness, the gut-deep dread that he would lose the only part of his life that mattered before he ever had the chance to tell her what she meant to him.

Just then, he heard a siren's wail. *Please. Please save her. Save our baby. I'll do anything, even—*

Even let her go, if that's what she wanted.

As the paramedics rushed in, Linc grasped Ivy's hand, pressed it to his lips and prayed.

MINUTES SEEMED HOURS as they waited at the hospital. Even Jeff's glares meant nothing to Linc as he stared out the window and made bargain after bargain with God to spare the woman who was his heart and the child they'd made together.

Finally, with quick, angry steps, the young man crossed the room. "If anything happens to her—"

Linc shook him off. "This won't help."

"I'm going to ask her to marry me," Jeff said.

Linc grabbed the front of Jeff's shirt and leaned in close. "She's mine," he growled. "She's carrying my baby."

"I'll take care of Ivy and her baby. She's too good for you." Jeff's eyes flashed in defiance.

Linc met his stare, but the memory of Ivy trying to get between them, of Ivy falling to the floor, made him loosen his grip. He glanced away. "You think I don't know that?" he said, voice raw.

Carl spoke behind them. "Jeff, stop it. Can't you see he's hurting, too?"

Jeff whirled. "Granddad, this is his fault. If he hadn't come here and ruined her life—"

Carl stood half a head shorter than his grandson, but he didn't back down. "Go on, boy. You leave this man alone. You're doing Ivy no good this way."

Linc could see love for the old man battling with a young man's fury. Jaw tight, finally Jeff nodded. With one last damning glare at Linc, he walked into the hall.

"He's right," Linc murmured. "I'm not good enough for her." He turned to face the old man's well-deserved accusation. "But I never meant to hurt her. I just couldn't figure out how to change what I'd started once I knew what she was like, how she could bring the sun to a dark day—" He looked away.

"Tell me why you did it, son."

Linc shrugged. "It doesn't matter."

"I think it does. I think we saw the real man when he wore blue jeans and drove a beat-up truck."

"You're wrong," Linc insisted. "You saw my Jag. Ivy saw my life in Dallas."

"Did she?" Carl said. "The man in jeans seemed real to me."

Linc stood silent for a long time.

"Talk to me, son," Carl urged.

"I didn't expect her." Linc stared sightlessly at the pale-green walls. "I thought Ivy Parker was some blue-haired crackpot who had nothing better to do than write letters. The first time I laid eyes on her, my chest got tight." He shook his head. "Flour on her cheek, a—" His voice cracked, but he kept going. "A baby in her arms. She was like nothing I'd ever encountered before, so damn beautiful a man wanted to reach out and make sure she was real."

He kept staring at nothing, seeing only Ivy. "She's not my type. I date women who eat nails for breakfast, women with their own lives who don't want a man to spend the night. I don't know the first thing about a woman who's got home and hearth written all over her, who belongs in some vine-covered cottage with babies and puppies."

Carl chuckled. "My Mildred thought she would go to New York City and live the high life. Me, I was going to marry my childhood sweetheart and we'd ranch. Then I go to this dance in Fort Worth and meet this girl, and we're all wrong for each other. But I couldn't get her out of my mind, and you know what? We weren't wrong, after all—just took some time to smooth out the rough edges. We had fifty-one years together. Happiest years of my life and hers, too." He clapped one hand on Linc's shoulder. "There's no accountin' for what the heart wants, boy. You think you're sure who you are and where you're goin', you're headin' there as fast as you can and then—*wham*. That one woman comes along, and maybe you don't recognize her at first or maybe you do. But the heart knows, and it won't leave you be.''

Linc shook his head. "I did lie to her, Carl. Lied to all of you.''

The old man squinted at him. "I understand that, but I'm thinkin' there's a reason why.''

"It doesn't matter. The harm's done. Ivy's lying in there hurt, and it all started with me.''

Carl shrugged. "You don't want to explain you don't have to, but I ain't got nothin' better to do if you want to talk.'' To emphasize his point, he sat down.

Then Linc realized that he wanted to explain to someone, though he didn't expect absolution. So he sat beside Carl and started talking—about his father and Betsey and Garner, about his life in Denver and the past he'd come back to confront too late to save his brother. About the site he'd found for Ivy's new café and how she'd thrown it back in his face like an insult.

Carl whistled. "You ain't too bright, are you, boy?''

Linc rubbed the spot between his brows. "Guess not.''

"See, boy, women got minds like a labyrinth, and a man ain't never goin' to figure out more than ten percent of them anyway, but I would have thought a man who could do all you've done would have a little more insight into what makes people tick, even if they're women." He shook his head. "Any fool could see that Ivy's put down roots in Palo Verde and that's that. Girl needs a home. Don't know why, exactly—Prudie's real closemouthed about Ivy's past, and Ivy herself could give the Sphinx a run for his money, but the girl's dug herself into Palo Verde deep. No amount of money goin' to change that. You want the girl, you got to take Palo Verde, too."

"I don't think she wants me, no matter how much I want her—" Linc broke off, seeing the doctor walking down the hall. He leaped to his feet. Not to shove everyone aside and demand to know her condition took all he had, but he'd forfeited all rights to Ivy when he'd made the choice to leave for Dallas without coming clean with her.

So while his heart thudded and he tried to decipher the doctor's expression, he forced himself to help Carl to his feet and stand back while the doctor spoke to Aunt Prudie.

When Aunt Prudie started crying, Linc's heart clenched.

She looked for Carl first, then Linc. "She's going to be all right. They don't know yet about the baby, but our girl's going to be all right."

Linc wanted to be grateful, and he was, but he

also knew somehow, deep in his bones, that if the baby was lost, something inside Ivy would die, too.

As would a part of him. He'd never thought about wanting babies, didn't know, in fact, that he could be any kind of father.

But now, when it was probably too late, he realized just how much he wanted this baby, how much he wanted to be linked with Ivy forever, even if she never forgave him.

Aunt Prudie walked slowly with the doctor, pausing for a minute to give Carl time to catch up.

Linc saw her searching the group and wondered if she sought him out.

But the sight of him would only upset Ivy, and she had suffered enough because of Linc Galloway.

Without a word, he headed into the night.

CHAPTER FIFTEEN

HE'D TRIED TO LEAVE Palo Verde, but he just couldn't go until he knew.

When the halls were quiet, he talked his way into the hospital and headed toward Ivy's room, certain she'd be asleep but needing to see her just one more time.

He stayed near the open door, unwilling to wake her as she lay there, so fragile, one hand splayed protectively over her belly.

Was his baby still there?

Let the little one live, he pleaded to the same God who had kept Ivy safe, praying as he'd never prayed in his life. *Don't take the baby from her. Please…I'll do anything.*

In the darkness, he waited, listening for what his part of the bargain must be.

Knowing no price was too high.

Wishing that he could go back to the beginning and do it all right this time.

A touch on his arm jolted him. Aunt Prudie stood there, studying his features. As if satisfied by what she'd seen, she placed her hand in the crook of his elbow. "Come with me, young man."

Linc cast a glance toward Ivy.

"Just out in the hall," she whispered. "We need to talk."

Though he wanted badly to stay with Ivy, he followed her aunt.

"Let's sit over there." She pointed.

He helped her into her chair.

"Sit down, young man," she said crisply. "This isn't an inquisition. I want to tell you about Ivy."

"It doesn't matter," he said. "I'm leaving."

"Giving up that easily?" Her eyebrows lifted. "I thought you were made of sterner stuff than that."

Her acerbic words couldn't pierce the lethargy despair had wrapped around him. He sat down on the edge of the seat. "It doesn't matter."

"I think it does. You see, Ivy lost a baby before," she said.

Linc nodded, looking at the floor.

"It just about killed her. She was only three months pregnant. She'd been a widow just under a week."

"God—" Linc rubbed his hands over his face. "She must have been devastated, losing the man she loved and then his baby."

Aunt Prudie snorted. "That worthless waste of

air? Oh, Ivy tried hard to make the marriage work, and she'd never have given up on it, left to herself. But the fool smashed himself and his latest girlfriend into a tree. Good riddance to bad rubbish, I say. But Ivy didn't take it that way. She blamed herself for not being enough woman for him. She took it hard, finding out the last five years of her life had been a lie."

"Then she lost the baby."

Aunt Prudie nodded. "Doctor told her it wasn't uncommon. One in four women miscarries the first time out. He told her there was no reason to think it would happen again, but Ivy lost a dream she'd had all her life. Until the night you and she—" She cleared her throat. "Well...she never cried, not once. I suspect she was afraid that if she started, she'd never stop. Girl's had a lot of sorrow in her short life—father deserting them, mother dying, sisters scattered to the winds. Ivy's always blamed herself for not being able to keep that family together, so she was doubly determined to make her new family work. Losing two families just took the life out of her. Our Ivy's not a quitter, though. She gave up on one dream but she started over in Palo Verde and made herself a new family out of old folks and babies and a broken-down town."

Linc leaned his elbows on his knees, running his hands through his hair as he stared at the floor.

"So when Ivy found out I'd lied to her and then I compounded it by offering her a site in Dallas, I couldn't have done anything much worse."

"Having a fiancée didn't work in your favor, either."

Linc's head jerked up. "I wasn't engaged when I was here. Betsey's my brother's widow, he killed himself. I left here suddenly beacuse my father was dying. When he asked me to marry Betsey, I thought I had to do it for my brother because I should have been there when—" He cleared his throat. "I promise you, I would never have gotten involved with Ivy if I'd been engaged."

Aunt Prudie nodded. "I believe you. Carl told me you're not engaged anymore."

Linc tried to smile. "Betsey set me free. She understood before I did."

"Understood what?"

"That I can't love her because I love Ivy."

Prudie studied him for a long time. "So what are you going to do now?" She glanced toward Ivy's door.

He stared at the door, but in his mind, he could see only Ivy in all the ways he'd known her: laughing, lecturing Carl, singing to a fretful child. "What's the best thing for Ivy?" he asked softly. "That's what matters now."

"Do you want this baby?"

He met her gaze. "More than anything in the world except that baby's mother."

Aunt Prudie peered at him, then nodded as if satisfied. "Then, don't give up. Ivy's going to need you."

At that moment, the malaise that had gripped him since he'd watched Ivy fall vanished. He'd always been a man of action, and a multitude of ideas fired his brain. He glanced at his watch, surprised to see that it was nearly midnight.

Damn the hour. He had calls to make.

"Let me take you home," he said, his gaze sliding toward the door of Ivy's room.

"In a minute." She nodded at the door. "Go ahead. It won't hurt."

As though entering a sacred space, Linc walked into Ivy's room and approached her bed. Needing badly to touch her, he settled for one lock of that golden hair, stroking it as gently as he wanted to stroke Ivy's face. He scanned down to the slender hand lying on her belly. With reverence, he placed his hand over hers, wanting with everything in him to protect baby and mother both.

"Linc?" Her voice was slurred with sleep.

He turned his head, afraid of the anger he deserved, but only confusion met him.

"What's happening? Where am I?" Then confusion gave way. Her hand tightened under his. "The baby—"

He cupped her cheek in one hand, clasping her other hand with his. "Still safe," he reassured her, and prayed that would continue.

He saw the moment she remembered and suspicion stirred.

"What are you doing here?" she asked.

"Shh," he soothed. "We'll talk later. Right now, you need to rest."

"But I—you—"

With unsteady fingers, he caressed her face, wishing he could pour out his heart, but unwilling to tax her strength. "Don't think about me now, Ivy. I'm not important. Our baby is what matters, our baby and you. Just sleep now, and when you're both back home, I have a story I need to tell you."

He saw when the battle ceded to her weariness. "I—what about your—Betsey?"

"Shh," he whispered. "Betsey's gone. She saw before I did that I'd be marrying the wrong woman."

Blue eyes searched his. "How can I trust you?"

His heart broke, and he hung his head. "Ivy, I promise—" He searched for the words, but words weren't up to the task.

A heaviness settled over him. He made himself meet her eyes, knowing it might be for nothing.

But Ivy had gone away from him, retreating into sleep.

Swallowing hard, Linc leaned over the bed and pressed a kiss to her forehead, smelling flowers and cinnamon but tasting only the bitter harvest of his deceit.

SHE'D DREAMED of Linc and their baby, a dark-haired boy who looked just like his father. When Ivy awoke, her first thought was panic.

"My baby?"

The nurse smiled and patted her hand. "Still there. You just take it easy. We'll be moving you soon."

"Moving me? Where?"

"To a private clinic in Dallas where you can be constantly monitored. Mr. Galloway is sparing no expense."

"I'm not going to Dallas." Just then, Ivy saw Aunt Prudie in the doorway, Carl behind her. "Aunt Prudie, you can't let Linc do this."

"Do what?"

"She says Linc wants me moved to Dallas. I won't go. I want to go home, Aunt Prudie. Carl, don't let him take me away."

"Now, honey," her aunt said. "It's just for a while. He wants you to have the best of care."

Ivy shot a glance at the nurse. "Do you work here?"

The woman shook her head. "I'm a private duty nurse. You're my only patient."

"Do I need to be in a hospital?"

The woman shook her head. "Not really. You just need to have complete bed rest for another week or so, to be sure. It's mostly a precaution."

"Do you have a family in Dallas?"

"No. I'm single."

"Cats? Dogs?"

"No."

"So you could do your job in Palo Verde just as well as anywhere?"

"If I have a cooperative patient, yes."

"Good," Ivy said. "I'm going home. I'll be the best patient you ever saw."

"Ivy, honey. Linc—" Prudie began.

"Don't talk about Linc to me. I'll take his nurse because I don't want anything to happen to this baby, but he's not running my life. He gave up the rights to that when he lied to me."

Carl spoke then. "Now, hold your horses, little girl. There's more to the story than that, and you should let him explain."

For a second, Ivy thought she remembered the press of Linc's mouth on her forehead and a strong hand clasping hers. A feeling of comfort and safety. "Where is he, then?"

Both Prudie and Carl looked discomfited. "Don't know. He left last night."

Sorrow stung her. She shook it off. "It doesn't matter. I need to rest to get back on my feet, and that's all I'm going to think about. I'm through dancing to any man's tune."

Aunt Prudie looked as though she wanted to speak, but she didn't. She and Carl traded sorrowful glances, but she held her peace.

"Good." Ivy nodded. "I'm going home to Palo Verde." If her heart ached knowing that Linc saw her only as a responsibility, well, that couldn't be helped. All that could matter now was her child.

BY THE NEXT MORNING, Ivy was already starved for activity. She felt fine. Only the knowledge of how crucial rest was for her baby's health kept her in bed.

So when the nurse told her Lora Lee had dropped by, Ivy fell on the news like a starving woman on a crumb of bread. "Oh, absolutely. Bring her in."

For a while they simply visited, Lora Lee catching her up on all the town doings. Carl's grandson had gone home. Sally's baby had said her first word. Mabel and Aunt Prudie were keeping the café running, but everyone missed Ivy.

"He loves you, you know," Lora Lee said, out of the blue. "Linc."

Ivy did a double take. "You can't know that."

"I do know that. Everyone does. You should give him a chance, Ivy. He's a good man."

Ivy stared at her. "After what he did?"

"I'm not saying he didn't make mistakes, but he came back, didn't he? He's paying for that nurse, and he's paying for Carl's home health nurse, too."

"He's got big bucks and a guilty conscience, that's all," Ivy insisted.

Lora Lee looked at her. "You're afraid, aren't you?" Wonder laced her tones. "I didn't know there was anything in the world that scared you."

"I'm not afraid. I'm mad. There's a difference."

"You wouldn't be mad if you didn't care. Don't you think you should give him a chance to explain? Ivy, life is short. We can't know what tomorrow will bring. Don't waste love when it's right there in your grasp."

Ivy remembered Lora Lee's lost love and couldn't be angry. "He doesn't love me, and anyway, it doesn't matter. He's gone again, and he won't be back."

"Oh, yes, he will," said a deep voice.

Ivy's gaze whipped to the doorway.

There Linc stood.

She had no idea what to say. The sight of him in the room where they'd spent the unforgettable night that had changed her life, the room where he'd left her and broken her heart—

Linc spoke, instead. "We need to talk, Ivy."

He smiled that smile that could knock a woman off her feet. Knock her into next week.

"Well, now…" Lora Lee glanced at Ivy as if to remind her of their conversation. "You and Ivy just talk now and get things all worked out."

"There's nothing to work out," Ivy muttered. "Lora Lee—"

But she was speaking to thin air. She could hear Linc saying goodbye in the front room. Ivy hoped he wouldn't be back.

She did. Really.

But she heard his deep voice in the next room, heard the nurse leave. Then he showed up again.

"We're alone," she accused.

"Yeah." He smiled, but his eyes were dark with worry. "The nurse says you're doing well, but I want to hear it from you. Any problems at all?"

"I'm fine," she snapped. "I want to talk about this yarn you're spinning for Lora Lee."

"I leave the yarn spinning to Carl. He's a better storyteller than I'll ever be."

Ivy could see it in his eyes when he heard what he'd said. He cursed softly and looked away.

"Look, Ivy—yes, I didn't tell you who I really was, but I never intended to hurt you. I expected you to be some blue-haired old lady who had nothing better to do than concoct foolish dreams and write letters, but instead you were—" He halted.

"I was what? A fool? Definitely. A dreamer? A—"

"The most beautiful woman I'd ever seen," he interrupted.

Ivy gave a decidedly unladylike snort. "I've seen Betsey, Linc. You can't expect me to believe that I'm more beautiful than she is."

"But you are," he insisted, coming to stand beside her bed. "It's more than just looks. You're beautiful in ways that will last long after beauty fades. You've got the heart of a lion, defending those you love. You have enough compassion for ten people. You spread sunshine and hope everywhere you go."

Ivy just stared at him, stunned by his words. Finally she spoke, her voice barely a whisper. "Then why, Linc? Why did you—why did we— You were engaged to her, and you—"

He lowered himself to the edge of the bed. "I wasn't engaged to her when I was here, Ivy. I would never do that to you or to her. But there were things going on that I couldn't tell you until I figured out the best way to deal with the tangle my brother had left.''

''Your brother who died?''

He looked at his hands. ''He didn't just die, Ivy. He killed himself.''

''Oh, Linc—''

He refused her sympathy. ''I wasn't there when he needed me. I had to do right for Betsey—these buildings were all she had left. I came here to help Betsey and my father, and then you made me care about a whole town full of people you're hell-bent on saving.'' He looked at her then. ''And you made me fall in love with you.''

She saw love in his eyes. There was nothing she wanted more, yet nothing that could scare her worse. Men didn't stay with her; they always found something missing.

His gray eyes held hers, full of pain and longing.

''How can I— Linc, I don't know who you are.''

''I didn't like lying to you, Ivy, not even at first.'' His voice roughened.

''Tell me. Make me understand.''

So Linc began to talk, and Ivy saw a picture emerging that broke her heart.

If she'd thought she loved him before, that was nothing to the emotion stirring her now. Her anger at him vanished. She wanted to wrap that boy in her love, wanted to be there beside the young man struggling all alone to make a new life.

Finally, he paused. "I didn't want to leave you, Ivy, but I had responsibilities I couldn't shirk. If I'd known about the baby, nothing could have kept me away, I swear it."

Euphoria fell to earth with a *thud*. "I've been in a marriage held together for the sake of a baby. It doesn't work."

"What?" He goggled as though she had two heads. "Ivy, the baby's not the reason I'm here. I mean, yes, I want it, but I'm here for you first. Ivy, I love you. Don't you understand that?"

"Don't," she said sharply. "It's too easy to say those words. People say them all the time, but they don't really mean them."

He stared at her for a long time, frustration tightening his features. "Ivy, how do I convince you—"

Then his eyes widened and he leaped to his feet. "Okay, how about this?" He stalked over to the desk in the corner of her room and grabbed a blank sheet of paper and a pen. While Ivy watched, frowning, he wrote quickly, filling most of the page. "We'll do this up in legalese later." He crossed back and handed it to her.

"What's this?"

"The deed to these buildings. I'm giving them to you."

"What?"

"You heard me." He knelt beside the bed. "That's where I went—to arrange to buy these buildings from Betsey." He clasped her hand. "Ivy, I know about your husband and the baby. I know about your dad."

"Aunt Prudie had no business—"

"She had every right—she loves you. A lot of people love you. I love you, too. I want to marry you and make a home with you and fill it with all the babies you want."

Tears pricked her eyes. It was all she'd ever wanted, but she couldn't believe it yet. "You'll get tired soon. My life isn't glamorous, and I don't want it to be. I don't fit in your world. Go back to Betsey. She's your type, and I'm not."

He studied her, his gaze tender. "Once, I agreed with you. I held on to an image of her that belonged to a boy. She's a good person and I'll always care about her, but we've grown in different directions. All that's between us is the past. I thought I needed to marry her to somehow make up for everything I didn't do for my brother, but she made me see that it's not enough. I'll want to help her as she finds her way, but as a friend, as the woman my brother loved. I don't love her, Ivy.

I love you. I need you, and I think you need me."
He leaned closer. "Give me a chance. You give
every stray dog a chance. Let me have one."

"It's no use. Men don't stay with me. I don't
know why." She was horrified to hear her voice
wobble.

"How do I make you believe me?" Linc held
one hand tightly, staring off into the distance. Suddenly, his head came up. "Okay, here's the deal.
Give me that paper."

She pulled it to her chest. "No. You can't take
it back."

"I'm not taking it back. Come on, Ivy, hand it
over. I'm not going to renege."

Very slowly, she relinquished it to him. He used
a spot on her nightstand to fill the back with his
bold handwriting, then signed that side, too.
"Here—" But he didn't let go yet. "Do you believe I'm a shrewd businessman?"

It didn't take a genius to recall his clothes, his
car, all the accoutrements of an expensive lifestyle.
"Yes, but what does that—"

"Well, I didn't get that way by making stupid
deals that I knew would cost me money. I've got
a deal for you, Ivy Parker. Let's see how good a
businesswoman you are."

She glanced at him sideways. "How?"

He gave her the paper. "I just committed to a

lifetime lease on one of the buildings, where I intend to move my operations.''

"Here?'' She gaped. ''To Palo Verde?

"That's right. But there's a stiff provision in the lease.''

Her gaze narrowed. ''What is it?''

"I pay no rent—''

Ivy frowned.

"As long as we remain in love and I make you happy. If not, the rent goes through the roof and I go broke.'' He held up one hand to quiet her. ''Not every-second-blissful kind of happy, mind you— no one could do that. Not 'I want that dress and I'm raising your rent if you don't get it for my birthday.' Not 'You didn't cook meat loaf the way I like it, so your rent goes up.' I'm not a superhero, but—'' He frowned. ''We can work out the language later—you know what I mean. As happy as any one man can make the woman he loves.'' Then he waited for her to respond.

She stared at him. ''You can cook meat loaf?''

"Ivy—'' he growled.

A grin wanted to emerge. ''I didn't know you could cook.''

One eyebrow lifted, and his eyes turned hot in a way that had her insides melting.

"I have all sorts of skills you don't know about

yet. That's why you have to become Mrs. Lincoln Galloway III, so I can show you."

"Mrs.—?"

"Okay, you don't have to take my name if you—"

"You really want marriage?"

He clasped her hand tighter. "That's the idea, sweetheart. I'd sign anything if it would convince you to marry me and let me spend the rest of my life making sure you never regret it."

"Oh, Linc…"

"And I want to help you look for your sisters. We'll get you so much family you'll be running for the hills to escape all of us."

"I don't need bribes."

"It's not a bribe—it's a promise." Then he sobered. "Please, Ivy. I never realized I needed a home until you. I'm no prize, I know that. I don't have much experience with love, but I promise you I'll give you everything that's in me." He looked at her then, yearning and love tangled up with worry. "Take a chance on me, make a home with me. You'll never regret it, I swear."

Ivy gazed at the man who'd already moved into her heart when she wasn't paying attention. He was the only father she wanted for this baby, the one man she could almost have the courage to believe would stay in her life. "When would you want to get married?"

His eyes went wide. His grin went wider. "This afternoon too soon?"

Ivy laughed. "I'm not getting married in my bed."

"Why not? Then we wouldn't have to travel for our honeymoon." All the darkness had fled from the eyes she'd so often seen haunted.

She clasped his head between her hands and pressed her mouth to his. The kiss quickly turned hot and sweet and hungry.

Then Linc broke away, his voice hoarse. "Forget that. We can find a judge this morning. The courthouse is right across the street."

Ivy grinned. "I'm not getting married until I can stand up."

"This baby's not going to be born out of wedlock, Ivy."

"I think I'm starting to feel a little unhappy," she warned. "I'm seeing dollar signs…"

Linc laughed, and it was sunshine after days of rain. "You want happy? I'll show you happy."

Carefully, he stretched out beside her on the bed and pulled her close, breath to breath…body to body…soul to soul….

Heart to overflowing heart.

EPILOGUE

IT WAS FALL before Linc had his way.

First there was the bed rest, then the dress Ivy was determined to make. Then Carl, who would give the bride away, wanted to be able to climb the necessary stairs. Then—until Linc and Aunt Prudie put their feet down—the wedding cake Ivy thought she should bake. By the time Ivy was satisfied that all the details were in place, she'd had to let out a seam in her gown. Some days Linc thought he might rip his hair out.

But, oh, she was worth the wait.

Finally, on a crisp, clear day in October, he stood on the steps of the Palo Verde courthouse, waiting to make Ivy his bride. No other place in town was big enough. The lawn overflowed with people wanting to share this joyous day with the woman who'd refused to let their little town die.

Linc saw the minister smile. A murmur swept through the crowd, and he turned to face his bride. People shifted to clear the way, and Linc's heart squeezed in his chest.

And there she was. Ivy, in the full-length dress she'd been denied when she eloped. Long sleeves, simple lines, it looked like the gown of a princess in a fairy tale. On the honey-blond curls tumbling down her back, she wore a wreath of flowers.

Linc had eyes for no one else. She moved to favor Carl's slower gait, stopping often in her progression to hug one person after another. Linc tried to stem his impatience, but it was hard.

At the front row she paused and presented a rose to Aunt Prudie. The two women hugged as Lora Lee wiped her eyes.

At last, Carl and Linc reached the steps, and Ivy's gaze locked on Linc's.

Home, he thought. *Wherever Ivy is, that's home for me.* How had he ever thought, after his banishment, that he hadn't needed a home? Ivy had lost her home not once but twice, yet her response had been to create home where she was. They'd taken such different roads in life.

Thank God they'd wound up in the same place.

Now he was building her a home on a hilltop, a home to house her dreams. Aunt Prudie would have her own little cottage on the grounds, they'd already agreed. The private detective he'd hired had a lead on one of Ivy's sisters, and Linc wouldn't stop until he'd found them both. Ivy wanted family, and he was happy to comply.

They'd fill their home to the rafters with family and babies and puppies—

And love. Most of all, love.

Suddenly, he couldn't wait any longer to begin. He left his place and descended the steps two at a time to meet her as the delighted crowd laughed.

"Linc," Ivy cautioned, "everyone's looking."

"I know." He grinned. "I'll handle it from here, Carl," he said, never taking his eyes off Ivy.

"Go ahead, son," Carl laughed. "She's a mite impatient herself."

Linc looked down into blue eyes that held enough love for a world. She was everything his heart had ever wanted, everything he'd thought he would never have. Throwing decorum to the winds, he pulled her close and kissed her hard. When her eyes were suitably hazed and emotion crowded his throat, Linc swept her up in his arms and started back up the steps.

Facing the minister, Ivy laughing and squirming but safe in his arms, Linc thought at that moment that life didn't get any better than this.

BUT HE WAS WRONG.

One chilly night in February, Ivy cuddled against him, weary but triumphant, mussed and more beautiful than his wildest dreams, Linc held her tightly with one arm as he cradled his daughter in the other, neither he nor Ivy able to stop staring at that tiny, precious face.

"She's beautiful," he said. "She looks just like you."

"She has your hair," Ivy pointed out. "And your eyes. She's nothing like me."

He looked into the face of the woman who'd changed his life. "As long as she has your heart," he said, "she has the best part of both of us."

* * * * *

*Watch for the stories of Ivy's sisters,
Caroline and Chloe, in upcoming
Superromances.*

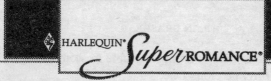

If you enjoyed what you just read,
then we've got an offer you can't resist!

Take 2 bestselling love stories FREE!

Plus get a FREE surprise gift!

Clip this page and mail it to Harlequin Reader Service®

IN U.S.A.	**IN CANADA**
3010 Walden Ave.	P.O. Box 609
P.O. Box 1867	Fort Erie, Ontario
Buffalo, N.Y. 14240-1867	L2A 5X3

YES! Please send me 2 free Harlequin Superromance® novels and my free surprise gift. After receiving them, if I don't wish to receive anymore, I can return the shipping statement marked cancel. If I don't cancel, I will receive 6 brand-new novels every month, before they're available in stores. In the U.S.A., bill me at the bargain price of $4.47 plus 25¢ shipping and handling per book and applicable sales tax, if any*. In Canada, bill me at the bargain price of $4.99 plus 25¢ shipping and handling per book and applicable taxes**. That's the complete price, and a savings of at least 10% off the cover prices—what a great deal! I understand that accepting the 2 free books and gift places me under no obligation ever to buy any books. I can always return a shipment and cancel at any time. Even if I never buy another book from Harlequin, the 2 free books and gift are mine to keep forever.

135 HDN DNT3
336 HDN DNT4

Name	(PLEASE PRINT)	
Address	Apt.#	
City	State/Prov.	Zip/Postal Code

* Terms and prices subject to change without notice. Sales tax applicable in N.Y.
** Canadian residents will be charged applicable provincial taxes and GST.
   All orders subject to approval. Offer limited to one per household and not valid to
   current Harlequin Superromance® subscribers.
® is a registered trademark of Harlequin Enterprises Limited.

SUP02   ©1998 Harlequin Enterprises Limited

Princes...Princesses...
London Castles...New York Mansions...
To live the life of a royal!

In 2002, Harlequin Books lets you escape to a
world of royalty with these royally themed titles:

Temptation:
January 2002—*A Prince of a Guy* (#861)
February 2002—*A Noble Pursuit* (#865)

American Romance:
The Carradignes: American Royalty (Editorially linked series)
March 2002—*The Improperly Pregnant Princess* (#913)
April 2002—*The Unlawfully Wedded Princess* (#917)
May 2002—*The Simply Scandalous Princess* (#921)
November 2002—*The Inconveniently Engaged Prince* (#945)

Intrigue:
The Carradignes: A Royal Mystery (Editorially linked series)
June 2002—*The Duke's Covert Mission* (#666)

Chicago Confidential
September 2002—*Prince Under Cover* (#678)

The Crown Affair
October 2002—*Royal Target* (#682)
November 2002—*Royal Ransom* (#686)
December 2002—*Royal Pursuit* (#690)

Harlequin Romance:
June 2002—*His Majesty's Marriage* (#3703)
July 2002—*The Prince's Proposal* (#3709)

Harlequin Presents:
August 2002—*Society Weddings* (#2268)
September 2002—*The Prince's Pleasure* (#2274)

Duets:
September 2002—*Once Upon a Tiara/Henry Ever After* (#83)
October 2002—*Natalia's Story/Andrea's Story* (#85)

Celebrate a year of royalty with
Harlequin Books!
Available at your favorite retail outlet.

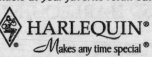

HARLEQUIN®
Makes any time special ®
Visit us at www.eHarlequin.com

HSROY02